Jody Gehrman

Triple
Shot
Bettys
in love

Dial Books

DIAL BOOKS
A member of Penguin Group (USA) Inc.
Published by The Penguin Group
Penguin Group (USA) Inc., 375 Hudson Street, New York, NY 10014, U.S.A.

Penguin Group (Canada), 90 Eglinton Avenue East, Suite 700, Toronto, Ontario, Canada
M4P 2Y3 (a division of Pearson Penguin Canada Inc.)
Penguin Books Ltd, 80 Strand, London WC2R 0RL, England
Penguin Ireland, 25 St. Stephen's Green, Dublin 2, Ireland
(a division of Penguin Books Ltd)
Penguin Group (Australia), 250 Camberwell Road, Camberwell, Victoria 3124,
Australia (a division of Pearson Australia Group Pty Ltd)
Penguin Books India Pvt Ltd, 11 Community Centre,
Panchsheel Park, New Delhi - 110 017, India
Penguin Group (NZ), 67 Apollo Drive, Rosedale, North Shore 0632,
New Zealand (a division of Pearson New Zealand Ltd)
Penguin Books (South Africa) (Pty) Ltd, 24 Sturdee Avenue, Rosebank,
Johannesburg 2196, South Africa
Penguin Books Ltd, Registered Offices: 80 Strand, London WC2R 0RL, England

Designed by Nancy R. Leo-Kelly
Text set in Weiss
Printed in the U.S.A.
1 3 5 7 9 10 8 6 4 2

Library of Congress Cataloging-in-Publication Data
Gehrman, Jody Elizabeth.
Triple Shot Bettys in love / Jody Gehrman.
p. cm.
Summary: Sixteen-year-old Geena spends a winter coping with a gorgeous new girl in town
who is after her boyfriend, Ben, her mother's return to dating, and her best friend Amber's
crush on an English teacher, while continuing to serve espressos at Triple Shot Betty.
ISBN 978-0-8037-3248-3
[1. Interpersonal relations—Fiction. 2. Dating (Social customs)—Fiction.
3. Friendship—Fiction. 4. High schools—Fiction. 5.Schools—Fiction.
6. Sonoma County (Calif.)—Fiction.] I. Title.
PZ7.G25937Tri 2009 [Fic]—dc22 2008030972

For my father,
who always believes in me

Thursday, December 18
4:15 P.M.

To: herolovespink@gmail.com
From: skatergirl@yahoo.com
Subject: Betty Reunion, Baby!

Hey Hero,
I know you come home for winter break tomorrow, which
renders this e-mail kind of unnecessary if not pathetic, but
I just have to give you a heads-up on the latest Sonoma
Valley High gossip, such as it is.

Did you know there's this new chick throwing a party
tomorrow night? You're invited, by the way. I haven't met her
yet, but her name's Sophie De Luca, and everyone's talking
about this bash. She hasn't even started school here, and
already she's planning social domination. I guess she knows
some locals, since she was born in Sonoma, but still. Her
family's been living in New York since she was five, and now
they're moving back here. Ben's known her since he was little,
and their families have stayed friends. Apparently they're
pretty tight.

Which is fine. Who, me, jealous? Ha! Just because I checked

out her pictures on Facebook and she's got scary gorgeous hair and spent last summer interning at <u>Mademoiselle</u> and clearly never had a zit in her life, you think I'm threatened? Pshaw!

Anyway, Cuz, enough about that—the important thing is you're coming home for two whole weeks and the Bettys will be together again. Connecticut's loss is our gain. Look out, oh ye seekers of caffeinated beverages. Ye shall taste the triple shot and ye shall be amazed!

Until tomorrow,
Geena

Friday, December 19

11:50 P.M.

The second I got to Sophie De Luca's Christmas party tonight I felt like a total mutant. We're talking major social anxiety of the palpitating heart variety.

I'd decided to skate there after work since I got off late. I had on my Triple Shot Betty tank top, jeans, and my favorite fleece hoodie. Usually I feel totally at home in this ensemble, but when I skated up to the house and saw two girls I didn't recognize out on the porch in little black dresses, I sensed a distinct suckieness creeping into my night. They looked like fashion models taking a break from the runway. Jewelry sparkled at their throats and they were both slender as reeds. When they saw me skate up, they gave each other that look—you know the one—like *Who's this pathetic loser and why is she breathing our air?*

I kicked my board up and caught it with one hand, then carried it up the steps. One of the girls let out a little snigger. I ignored them and rang the bell.

A striking girl with alabaster skin swung open the huge door, and suddenly everything about me felt doubly, disastrously *wrong*. She was more glam and glossy than anyone I've ever seen outside of a shampoo commercial. Her dark hair hung below her shoulders in a slick, silky mane. She had on this black sequined cocktail dress that made her legs look about four miles long. Her icy blue eyes assessed me quickly, darting down to my Pumas and back up to my face. I felt like a mangy mutt caught peeing on her doorstep.

"You must be Geena." Her mouth smiled, but her eyes stayed cold.

"Yeah," I said. "How'd you guess?"

She glanced at my skateboard. "Benedict said you were skating over."

Benedict? Is that what she calls Ben? I felt sicker and sicker every second.

"I'm Sophie. So glad you could make it."

"Thanks for inviting me," I mumbled, then instantly regretted it. After all, it was Ben who had asked me to come, not Sophie. "Sorry I'm so underdressed. I came from work."

"Not a problem. Come on in."

She led me through the elegant stone foyer down a hallway lit with muted sconces. When we reached the sunken living room, I took in the scene. A massive Christmas tree sparkled in the corner, all white lights and tasteful, bejeweled ornaments. A wall of windows gave the impression that the room hung suspended over Sonoma Valley, with a large, light-festooned deck extending outward like the bow of a great ship. Cream-colored tapers in silver candelabras draped the scene in tawny hues and dramatic shadows.

There were like forty or fifty people there. I only knew about half of them, and the other half looked older, maybe college students. Everyone (no joke, *everyone*) was dressed up—or at least, dressed up compared to me.

"Drinks are over there." Sophie pointed to a large, stainless steel bar near the Christmas tree, where Marcy Adams stood pouring martinis. "There's plenty of appetizers in the other room. Should I take your . . . sweatshirt?"

"Oh. No. I'm fine." I pulled my hoodie a little tighter around me, feeling about seven. "Thanks."

"No problem."

I spotted Amber's flaming red hair across the room. "I'm going to go say hi." I made a beeline for my friend, anxious to escape Sophie's icy, appraising stare.

Amber was talking to PJ. "What's up?" I said. She spun around at the sound of my voice and wrapped her arms around me, spilling a little of her drink on my sweatshirt in the process. She wore a bright paisley dress with sequins at the neckline. "Geena! You made it!" Then she lowered her voice to an ominous whisper. "Just in time."

"Yo," PJ said, touching his backward baseball cap in a sort of salute. Even he was dressed up in a black silk shirt and baggie black chinos. "How's it going?"

"I'm okay." I was distracted by Amber, though, who had this weird look on her face. "What do you mean, 'just in time'?"

Peals of silvery laughter caught our attention from across

the room. Sophie. I did a double take when I saw that the source of her hilarity was none other than Ben. She squeezed his arm with one hand and leaned toward him as if knocked off balance by his devastating sense of humor. Her dark, silky hair spilled over her shoulder enticingly.

Amber murmured, "Your boyfriend's been hijacked by the new girl."

Her words stirred a torrent of butterflies in my belly, and not just for the obvious reasons. The truth is, "boyfriend" still isn't a term I'm all that comfortable with. I mean, yeah, I've been seeing Ben for about five months, but somehow whenever someone calls him my boyfriend, I still feel this weird little fluttery burst of panic in the pit of my stomach. It's not that I don't like him—I totally do—but being a full-on couple comes with all this baggage I'm not sure I'm ready for.

"How does Ben even know her?" PJ asked, staring across the room at Sophie's sequined ass with a look of unabashed lust.

"She used to live here when she was little," I told him.

Amber rolled her eyes. "The point is, she's flirting with Ben big-time. Not good, G. You got to get in there, show her your roundhouse kick to the head."

PJ laughed. "I'd pay good money to see that. I'm going to go get another drink, then get a good seat!" With that he left us for the bar, but I could see his eyes lingering still on Sophie's slender, partly exposed back.

"Geebs!" Hero ran over and tackled me with a hug. We jumped up and down, happy to see each other, until we realized everyone was staring at us. She backed off and sipped daintily from her bottle of Perrier, smoothing her slick blond bob. She looked cute in her pink cashmere twinset, though I couldn't help noticing that even Hero couldn't compete with Sophie in the vogue department.

Another explosion of laughter came from Sophie's corner of the room, and I willed myself to stare at my own hands rather than swiveling my head in her direction.

"What's happening?" I asked through clenched teeth. "I can't look."

"Oooh, she's pulling the old Popsicle trick," Amber informed me.

"What's that?" My stomach clenched.

"You know, take a food item—in this case, a couple of olives on a toothpick—then lick and nibble suggestively."

Hero sucked in her breath. "Oh my God, you're right!"

I couldn't help it; I had to look. Sure enough, Sophie was twirling the skewered olives against her bee-stung, glossy lips, a look of rapt pleasure in her eyes. Just as she bit into one, she glanced in my direction. Was it my imagination, or did she actually bare her teeth at me? I swallowed hard and looked away.

"*Feliz Navidad!*" Suddenly the stofers exploded into the room, trailing clouds of skunky smoke. Stofer is what Amber and I call the stoner-surfers, mostly because it's a lot easier to say. Dog Berry sauntered forward in the lead, his scruffy, white-blond hair uncombed as usual. Behind him were Virg Pickett and George Sabato, their eyes glazed. All three wore their usual surfer boy pothead attire: sweats, T-shirts, Uggs. Finally, I wasn't the only one underdressed. They looked like crusty, unwashed stowaways stumbling into the *Titanic's* grand ballroom.

This would be interesting.

Everyone watched as Sophie glided across the room, her sparkling martini glass held aloft in one hand. "Greetings," she said. "Welcome to *chez moi*. And you are . . . ?"

"Heh, heh, heh," Dog chuckled. "I'm Dog. This is George, and that's Virg."

"I'm Sophie. The drinks are over there," she told them, waving a hand at the bar. "*Mi casa es su casa.*"

The room went back to buzzing with conversation. Crisis averted. Instead of relief, I couldn't help feeling a distinct pang of disappointment. Not only was our hostess rich, thin, chic, and strikingly beautiful—apparently she was also open-minded when it came to bong-a-lots. Even though I like the stofers, it would have been much more reassuring if she'd pulled a snotty New York socialite move and thrown them out on their baked butts.

"Hey, Sloane." I turned around and found myself looking right into Ben's shy, smiling face. He was as yummy as usual—maybe even more so. He wore an olive green sweater and black cargo pants. His short brown hair looked like it had just been cut, and his dark eyes sparkled in the candlelight.

"Hi." I tried to make my voice sound normal, but just standing near him sent a jolt of excitement straight through me.

He reached out a hand and tugged gently on one of my braids. "Didn't even know you were here yet."

"Well, here I am," I answered lamely.

"Here you are." He leaned over and kissed me on the lips. Really, it was more a tease than a kiss—a brushing of lips, a lingering closeness, yet somehow it made me all goose-pimpled. After a couple of seconds I pulled away, awkward and embarrassed. I just don't do public displays of affection very well. I noticed Hero and Amber melting off into the crowd.

"Everything okay?" He studied me so intently, I wondered with mild panic what my expression was giving away this time. I have no poker face. Every possible emotion—especially the most embarrassing variety—leaks out through my traitorous pores.

"Yeah, sure. I just feel like a total slob." I glanced down at my faded jeans and sneakers. "Everyone else is dressed up."

He put a hand on my waist and pulled me closer. "You look great."

"Oh, right."

"You do!" He pressed his face into my hair. "You smell so good."

I giggled. Ben's very in touch with his nose. That's one of the things I've had to get used to since we started dating: being sniffed all the time. "What do I smell like?"

"Mmmm . . ." He closed his eyes and considered. "Like nighttime, Christmas, and espresso beans."

I covered my mouth. "Do I have coffee breath?"

"No! You smell like the coffee section in the grocery store— that really delicious, freshly ground, dark, exotic smell."

"I guess that's one perk to being a minimum wage espresso wench—free perfume."

He laughed. By now he stood behind me, his arms wrapped all the way around me, his mouth right next to my ear. We were definitely in the PDA arena again, but the warmth of his body felt too good to even consider pulling away.

"I missed you, Geena."

From across the room, I could see Sophie clinking glasses

with PJ, laughing that throaty, sophisticated laugh of hers. "You didn't seem to be missing me a few minutes ago."

"What do you mean?"

"You and Sophie seemed to be having a great old time."

He turned me around, grasped my shoulders, and lowered his chin to give me one of his laser-intense stares. "We were in the same playgroup as babies, okay? We're just old friends."

"Oh, I know. That's cool." The last thing I wanted was to morph into some sort of girlzilla, plaguing him with nagging, suspicious questions. I tried to change the subject, but somehow the words that popped out were, "She's gorgeous."

"You think?" He glanced over at her, his expression nonchalant. "I guess she's pretty."

"Very glam." *Next to her I feel like a pygmy with a lisp,* I thought, but I didn't want to highlight my own inadequacies.

"She's always been into clothes. Even when we were little. Her life's mission is to be editor-in-chief at *Vogue.*"

"Noble calling." Snarky, snarky. I couldn't help it. Her laughter continued to haunt me from across the room, though I refused to turn around. Trying to sound less bitter, I added, "She obviously has great taste. I wish I had half her style."

"No offense, Sloane, but I never pegged you for a fashion plate."

"What?" I said defensively. "I like nice clothes."

"Long as you can skate in them, right?" He was teasing me, but I wasn't really in the mood. It made me slightly nauseous to know Ben saw me as a tomboy when Sophie De Luca was so fabulously the opposite: a high-maintenance, runway-worthy glamazon.

Before I could think of a reply, I noticed Ben's gaze had

moved from my face to some point over my shoulder. This sounds like I'm being a drama queen, but I seriously felt a chill against my back, as if someone had opened a window and let a gust of cold air in. I turned around and saw Sophie slinking toward us, her glossy lips stretched wide in a smile that showed off her cosmetically perfect teeth.

"You lovebirds having fun?" she asked in a coy, ironic tone that made the question impossible to answer. Luckily, she didn't wait for a response. "Geena, I'm so glad you could make it. Ben's told me so much about you."

"Has he?"

"Yee-ees." She drew the word out into two syllables, all the while batting her thick, dark lashes. "We've known each other for years."

"Yeah, he told me that." I instinctively took a step toward Ben and wrapped an arm around his waist. "Are you glad your family moved back to Sonoma?"

She sipped her martini, then ran her tongue over her teeth in a thoughtful way, as if my polite, offhand inquiry required serious contemplation. "Well, it's nothing like New York, of course, but Sonoma has its charms." Her tone implied that Sonoma's "charms" were primitive but quaint, like snake handling or starting a fire with a couple of sticks. "Benedict tells me you work in a coffee shop—is that right?"

"Sort of. Triple Shot Betty's. It's a drive-through espresso stand."

"I wouldn't last a second—I'm so claustrophobic." She turned again to Ben. "Remember that time when our parents took us to the county fair? I completely lost it on the Ferris wheel!"

She launched into a long anecdote, her eyes locked on Ben the whole time. She punctuated every other sentence with a husky laugh. I found myself mesmerized by her eyebrows; they were so perfectly shaped, so expertly groomed. They gave her the cool, polished elegance of a starlet from the forties. I promised myself to experiment with tweezing the second I got home.

"Yeah," Ben chuckled when her story finally ended. "Good times."

"Well, anyway, I'll leave you two. Just wanted to say hi. And Geena, I'm really glad you came, especially since you had to come straight from work—what a drag!" Her eyes flitted for a microsecond over my outfit before landing again on my face with a thin smile.

"Yeah, thanks for—" I almost said "inviting me" again, but saved myself just in time. ". . . having me."

As she walked away, almost as an afterthought, she grabbed Ben's arm and kissed him quickly on the cheek. Kissed him! Where did she think we were, Paris? Ben, who looked nearly as startled as me, blushed. She just kept walking, apparently oblivious.

"What was that about?" I asked, feeling distinctly queasy.

"Oh, that's just Sophie," Ben said. "She's a flirt. It doesn't mean anything."

By then Sophie had reached the other side of the room, where Marcy freshened her martini. There, leaning against the bar, with at least two-thirds of the guys in the room staring at her sequined butt, she threw a quick glance over her shoulder—a quick, feline look of challenge intended for me alone.

Saturday, December 20

7:40 P.M.

Tonight I found my mother doing some sort of samba while she fried ground beef and onions.

"What's up with you?" I asked.

She beamed at me over her shoulder. *Beamed at me*. I haven't seen my mother beam since . . . well, since way before Dad left, actually.

"Are you going to answer?" I asked, suspicious.

"I'm just in a good mood."

"Yeah, but *why* are you in such a good mood?"

She sambaed over to a bottle of red wine on the counter and poured herself a glass. "Something good happened, that's all."

"Something good like . . . ?"

She sipped her vino, then pressed her lips together in an I've-got-a-secret-I'm-dying-to-tell-you smile. In that moment, she could have passed for a teenager. "Someone asked me out."

I knew I should be happy for her. Instead, visions of creepy stepfathers paraded through my brain, each one pausing to leer suggestively for the mug shot. It was one thing to put up with Dad's arm charm, Jen, on weekends and holidays; it was something else entirely to consider harboring the enemy right here at home.

"Geena," Mom said, "don't look like that . . ."

"Don't look like what?"

"Like you just took a bite of my pâté."

Somehow, her stab at humor only made me more sullen.

"Listen, it's just a date, okay?" She came over and touched my cheek. "It's not like he's moving in or anything."

"What's his name?" I asked, staring at my shoes.

She paused. "You promise you won't laugh?"

I nodded.

"Mungo MacMartin."

A nervous caw of laughter escaped before I could slap my hand over my mouth. "You are kidding, right?"

She shook her head. "I know, it's a weird name, but he's Scottish. I think it's kind of cute."

When I cocked an eyebrow, she hurried to shift the focus away from his cartoonish moniker. "He's a really nice guy— or he seems like it, anyway. He coaches the girls' soccer team at Sonoma State."

"That's cool." My tone was noncommittal.

"Geena?"

I looked at her. "Yeah?"

"Try to keep an open mind, okay? Nothing like this has happened for me in ages, and it would really help me if you could just . . ." She trailed off.

"Disappear?" I supplied helpfully.

"No!" She looked horrified. "How can you even say that? No, just try not to hate him before you meet him, that's all."

I looked back at my shoes. She pulled me into a hug. I didn't want to be a brat, I really didn't. If I was already living at Yale, a good three thousand miles away, my reaction would be totally different. But she had to understand that any man who entered the picture now was bound to be a threat. Even if he was the nicest, most congenial Mungo on the planet, his entry into our home, which was still rocking from Dad's departure, couldn't be taken lightly.

Mom leaned away from me, her arms still wrapped around me, and tilted her head in a quizzical way. "What are you thinking?"

I shrugged. "Soccer coach, huh? Does he wear a whistle?"

"I doubt he'll wear it to dinner," she joked. Her face lit up in a luminous smile, and I thought, *If he hurts her, I'll kill him.*

I went to the fridge to hunt for something edible. There wasn't much. I managed to find a lemon yogurt that wasn't too far past its expiration date. As I shoveled spoonfuls into my mouth, I contemplated this new development. Mom was on the market again—she was experiencing the thrill of the hunt. Even if it was unnatural and wrong for old people to be indulging in lustful thoughts, I shouldn't begrudge her the sparkle of a new romance, should I? Besides, maybe if she remembered what it was like, she'd be less uptight about Ben and me.

"So, when's this big date?" I asked.

"Monday night."

"What are you doing?"

"Going out to dinner. He'll pick me up here around seven. Will you be home?"

This looked like the perfect moment to test my Mom-Gets-Some-I-Get-Some Hypothesis. "Don't think so. Ben and I are going to the movies."

"Okay. Another time, then."

I decided to push my theory a little further. "I'm not sure when I'll be home."

She shook some garlic salt into the pan, then dumped

a bunch of spaghetti sauce on top of that. It sputtered and hissed maniacally. She frowned and turned the heat down.

"Is that okay?"

"Hmmm?" she asked absently.

"I might be home late Monday."

"Isn't it a school night?"

"Earth to Mom—Christmas break!"

"Yeah, okay." She started a pot of water boiling for pasta.

I couldn't resist adding, "Maybe I'll just stay the night at Ben's."

Her head swiveled in my direction with enough speed and elasticity to give her an *Exorcist* air. "What did you just say?"

I laughed. "Nothing. Never mind."

Well, at least I'd established how much I could milk the Mungo factor.

Sunday, December 21

9:45 P.M.

This morning I was like, "Triple Shot Bettys Reunion! Break out the caffeine, baby, because the Wonder-Trio is back!" Amber, Hero, and I were all set for an extra-long shift at TSB—the first time we've worked together since Hero left for boarding school in August. Amber and I needed extra cash so we could celebrate the birth of Christ by wracking up debt on crappy consumer goods (table that rant for another day). Hero, of course, didn't need a dime, but she wanted to hang with us, so we all crammed into the closet-sized espresso stand and cranked up the tunes.

We'd been having a massively fabulous time for a couple

hours when I saw something that made me officially hate the world. Sophie De Luca drove up in a Mercedes convertible. It was silver, sleek, shiny, and flawless just like her. Marcy Adams sat in the backseat with PJ and Dog Berry. Riding shotgun was none other than Ben Bettaglia.

Cue screeching alarms: reet, reet, reet!

"Hello, Geena." Sophie beamed up at me, her face half hidden by an enormous pair of Gucci sunglasses. Her smooth tone did little to mask the smug triumph just under the surface.

"Hey, Sophie. Nice ride." I had to work very hard at controlling my expression.

"It's Sophie's birthday today," Ben informed me. "Look what she got!" He gestured at the car, obviously impressed.

"Benedict!" Sophie reached over and slapped his arm playfully. "Don't go telling everyone! People will think I'm spoiled."

"Oooh, yeah," I said. "Wouldn't want that, would we, *Benedict?*"

Behind me, Amber made a subtle gagging sound.

Sophie touched up her perfect lips in the rearview mirror with a tube of MAC lipstick. "I'll take a double macchiato, please. What do you guys want? I'm paying."

Everyone else ordered. I gritted my teeth and jabbed violently at the cash register while Hero and Amber went to work making the drinks. Hero shot me burning looks of sympathy. Amber leaned in close and whispered, "You just say the word, and I'll unleash the power of Macchiato con Tabasco."

"Tempting, but no," I muttered.

"Fine. Wimp."

I turned back to the window. "That'll be sixteen fifty."

Sophie reached for her purse, but Ben (a.k.a. "Benedict") reached across her and handed me a twenty instead.

"Keep the change," he said, grinning up at me as if his three-dollar-fifty-cent tip would surely make up for the sickly sludge of jealousy coursing through my veins.

Amber delivered their drinks, all the while giving Sophie major stink-eye.

Ben, genius that he is, sensed the tension. He threw me a look that was part apology, part you're-my-girl, and said, "Call me when you get off."

As they drove away, I found myself staring after them, hating the sight of Sophie's gorgeous dark hair fanning out behind her in the breeze.

Amber spoke first. "G, don't even trip. Ben's so not into her."

"Oh, yeah," I sneered, "why *would* he be? She's only perfect in every way. Wait—weren't you just warning me on Friday that she's trying to steal him?"

"Oh, she's trying to steal him, all right," Amber told me. "But Ben's all about you. He won't look twice at that skank."

"I'm sure they're just friends," Hero added, sipping primly at her soy chai.

Despite their reassurances, I couldn't ignore the queasy feeling that clung to my insides the rest of the day.

Monday, December 22
11:45 P.M.

Ben picked me up tonight in his faded yellow Volvo. That thing's so rust-eaten and dilapidated, it's like every puff of exhaust is sure to be its last; I believe it dates back to the Mesozoic period.

But here's the weird thing: Two seconds after he'd pulled up, just as I was applying a little lip gloss, I glanced out the window and thought I was seeing double. Parked right behind him in the driveway was another prehistoric Volvo, this one an ugly, mixed-too-many-colors-together brown.

Suddenly Mom was peering over my shoulder, smelling of super-charged lavender. "Look! Our guys are talking."

Ben had climbed out of the driver's seat and was now conversing with the other Volvo owner amiably, his hands shoved in his pockets. I decided to ignore the "our guys" comment, since it was just a little too sugary-cute for my taste.

"That must be Mungo," I said, trying to keep my voice neutral.

She nodded, then started fussing with her hair, using the window as a mirror. "What do you think?"

I studied the man in our driveway. He was a couple inches shorter than Ben, with pale, thinning hair and a pinkish face. He was wearing a beige cotton sweater and crisp new jeans. The look didn't scream mother-murdering-psycho-killer, but then, you can't be too careful these days.

"Seems okay from here."

She snorted. "Try to restrain your enthusiasm."

"What do you want me to do? Fling myself at him screaming Daddy?"

"Geena." There was enough hurt in those two syllables to make me regret my acerbic tone.

"Sorry," I said. "He looks nice. Really."

"How's this outfit? Okay?"

I turned around and surveyed my mother. She had on a knee-length denim skirt, a red cashmere cowlneck sweater, and red patent-leather slingbacks. Her auburn hair was glossy, blown dry into a smooth shoulder-length bob. I could tell she'd spent some time on it, maybe even gotten some highlights yesterday at the salon. I had to admit, she looked better than I'd seen her look in ages. If Mungo was responsible, I should at least make an effort to be civil.

"You look totally great," I said.

She snickered nervously. "Seriously?"

"Yeah, seriously."

The doorbell chimed then, and we froze, staring at each other for a panicky beat. Since Dad left last year, we'd inhabited a veritable boy-free zone. Suddenly there were two flesh-and-blood males on our doorstep, demanding entrance.

"You want me to get it?" I asked.

Her eyebrows arched. "Would that be weird?"

"I live here, don't I?"

She nodded. "Okay, you get it. I'm going to down a swig of wine." She scurried toward the kitchen, then stopped. "Not that I'm implying alcohol is an acceptable remedy for nerves."

I waved her away and headed for the foyer. Checking briefly in the hallway mirror for nose shine or stray hairs, I took a deep breath and swung the door open.

"Hi, Ben." I took in his familiar face before letting my gaze slide over to the man next to him. "You're Mungo, right?"

He offered a pink, freckled hand, and I shook it.

"That's right. I suppose you're Geena."

"Yeah."

"Nice to meet you."

The Scottish accent threw me a little, though it shouldn't have—Mom said something about that, didn't she? Anyway, I liked it. He sounded like someone from *Trainspotting*. I wondered fleetingly if he was a heroin addict, but he looked far too pink-cheeked and earnest for that. Then again, Ewan McGregor looked positively edible in that movie, and he was a total junkie.

I let them in and headed automatically for the kitchen; the second I passed through the archway, though, something trés bizarre happened. There was Mom in her underwear—an electric blue *thong*, of all things—flapping her arms madly in the universal *do not enter* signal. I sucked in my breath, shot her a quick *WTF* look, and did an abrupt about-face, narrowly avoiding a head-on collision with Mungo.

"Sorry," I mumbled. "I forgot—the floor's still wet in here. Why don't we go to the . . ." But where could we go? Our kitchen and living room are connected, so all that left me room-wise was bedroom, office, closet, or bathroom. A hilarious vision of Ben, Mungo, and me kicking it on the edge of the tub almost set me off on a violent giggling fit. I pursed my lips and started leading them back down the hall, retracing our steps. "Why don't we wait out on the porch? I'm sure Mom will be out in a minute."

"Uhh, okay." I could hear the confusion in Ben's voice, but he knew better than to question me openly when I was this high-strung.

"It's such a nice evening," I trilled as we stepped out onto the front porch. Actually, a dense fog had rolled in and the dank air felt bone-chilling, but I ignored this and gestured expansively to the porch swing. "Please, have a seat. Can I get anyone a drink? Mungo, you want a beer or a glass of wine?"

"Wouldn't mind a beer, if you've got one." He looked cheered by the prospect.

"Ben? Soda or something?"

Ben shook his head. "No, thanks."

I made a beeline for the kitchen. Soon as I walked in, Mom turned to me in bug-eyed horror and we bent our heads together in a whispered conference.

"What are you doing?"

"What did you tell him?" I noticed she had her skirt in one hand and a spray bottle filled with yellowish liquid in the other.

"That my mother's a lunatic and she's prancing around the kitchen half-nekkid!"

Her hands seized my shoulders in a death grip. "You didn't?!"

I rolled my eyes. "Please, I have a rep to protect here too, remember? You mind explaining . . . ?" I gestured at her attire.

"I went to pour the wine, but I was nervous and it spilled. Then I tried to get the stain out, but I grabbed the wrong bottle and bleached it instead." She held up her skirt, now sporting a fist-sized white splotch.

Isn't the upside to aging supposed to be acquired wisdom? At that moment, my mother looked about as wise as a fourth grader who'd peed her pants.

"Why didn't you just run and change?" I asked.

"I started to, but then you guys were in the hall. I was trapped!"

I massaged my forehead with one hand. "They're outside now. Go get something on."

She nibbled her lip; otherwise, she didn't move.

"What now?" I demanded.

"Geena, what if I can't do this?"

"Do what?"

"*This!*" She shook her ruined skirt in the air.

"Get dressed?"

"No, date! I haven't done this since I was your age."

"Mom, I hardly think this is the time or place." My patience was nearly spent.

"What do I *wear?*" she whined. "I spent two days deciding on this outfit."

I eyed the blue thong. "Apparently."

She slapped my arm and dashed for the bedroom. I listened to the sound of her bare feet on the hardwood floor. But they stopped. Very suddenly. Bad sign.

"Hi, Ben," she said. "I was just . . . oh, never mind."

I cringed and peeked around the corner in time to see her practically diving for the bedroom door. And then she was gone.

Geriatric types should definitely be denied access to Victoria's Secret catalogs.

Ben looked at me. "Um . . ."

"Yeah. Don't even ask. You want to blow this joint?"

"Geena, why was your mom—?"

"What did I just say?"

"Don't ask."

"And what are you doing?"

He hung his head. "Asking."

"So you want to go?"

He gestured at the front porch. "Wouldn't that be kind of rude?"

"It's not like we're going on a double date!"

"You didn't even get him his beer."

He was right, of course. Which totally irked me. "Fine. We'll babysit the elderly for two more minutes. Then we're out of here."

"Fair enough."

I popped back into the kitchen, opened a Corona, poured it into a glass, polished off the two sips that wouldn't quite fit, and followed Ben back out to the front porch. Poor Mungo looked baffled as he hunched over on the swing, shivering in his thin cotton sweater.

"Here's your beer," I said. "You want to come in?"

He took the glass from me, his expression grateful if still a little perplexed, and followed us back inside, this time to the living room. I was just about to announce that Ben and I had to take off when Mom swept into the room laughing a laugh I'd never heard come out of anyone, let alone my own mother. She made her entrance wearing caramel-colored suede jeans and a white blouse so sheer, you could see her lace-trimmed cami underneath. As she glided in on her high-heeled boots, she emitted this giggle that was sweet and light as little clouds of powdered sugar.

Mungo had barely sat down; he sprang up again, reaching out to take her hands. I could tell right then he was totally into her. He just had that *look*, you know? Not like a wolfish leer—more like *Marry me, radiant goddess.* I wasn't prepared for that.

All at once I needed to escape. It was just way too confusing seeing my primary caregiver first in a thong, and then being worshipped by a pink-faced Mungo. My parents have only been divorced a little over a year, and in that time they've gone from virtually sexless beings who maybe went for a peck on the cheek now and then to raging pheromone factories. Isn't this supposed to be my time to horrify *them* with my burgeoning sexuality?

"We've gotta go." I grabbed Ben's hand and bolted for the door. Mom and Mungo called their good-byes, but faintly, like they weren't really sorry to see the last of us.

After getting safely strapped into Ben's old Volvo and headed for the movies, I said, "You know the problem with parents today?"

He smirked. "I've got a feeling you're about to tell me."

"All those drugs they took in the eighties convinced them they're capable of time travel."

"Time travel?" Ben sprayed the window with wiper fluid and the blades struggled to chase each other across the glass.

"They think they can just wave their arms and be teenagers—without acne or a curfew. It's revolting."

"If you say so, Sloane."

That kind of made me mad. I mean, did he agree, or not? Obviously not—people never say "If you say so" when they actually mean it. "So you think I'm being stupid?"

"Not at all." He looked alarmed, which mollified me slightly.

"But you don't agree with my theory."

He considered. "My parents definitely have no illusions about time travel."

"Not all parents!" I blew my hair out of my eyes. "I didn't say *all*—"

"But I wish they did," he said. "It would make things a lot more interesting."

"Ha!" I shook my head. "You have no idea."

Wednesday, December 24
10:20 P.M.

Okay—can I just say?—this is so not cool. It's one thing to be from a broken home. I've already got that strike against me, but half of America does too, so whatever. What's unforgivable is being subjected to Christmas Eve with your divorced parents and their—eww! Dare I even write the word?—*lovers*.

How damaged am I by this evening?

Very, very damaged.

First, I want to report that things are moving way too fast on the Mom and Mungo front. If I went from hardly knowing a guy to inviting him over for important family functions within the span of four days, Mom would sit me down for a little tête-à-tête about the dangers of "rushing things," I guarantee it. Apparently, these rules don't apply to the over-forty set. She and the Mungo act like they've been together for decades rather than hours.

And then, buoyed by her victory over a loveless future—or maybe just giddy because she's finally getting some—Mom decided at the last second to invite Dad and Jen over for dinner. Never mind that I was perfectly happy having two Christmases, one here, and another at Uncle Leo's with Dad.

Now, purely for my benefit, I get to spend Christmas Eve with both of my parents at once—oh, and also with their respective sex partners.

Joy to the world.

I knew the emotional scarring was about to begin the second we all gathered around the dining room table. Jen sat so close to Dad she might as well have been in his lap, and her form-fitting dress revealed cleavage about as subtle as a blow to the head. Mungo looked even more eraser-pink than usual; was it my imagination, or did his gaze keep drifting to Jen's *décolletage? Quelle* disgusting! Mom and Dad haven't been in the same room for more than ten minutes since the divorce, so they were both edgy and smiling way too wide. As we picked at Mom's barely edible soufflé and ambitious-but-weird spinach and pomegranate salad, the small talk about the winter weather in our respective parts of the world petered out, and we found ourselves adrift in a queasy silence.

I don't know what made me feel responsible for taking action. It so wasn't my fault that this was happening! Somehow, though, with the twisted logic that is family drama, I felt obligated to resurrect the conversation.

"Hey, remember that Christmas we spent at Orion and Jackie's house?" Orion and Jackie were these family friends from my parents' hippie days. They grew pot in their backyard and drove a station wagon plastered in bumper stickers that said things like "Visualize Whirled Peas."

Mom shot a sideways glance at Dad. "Sure. You were what—eight?"

"Uh-huh. Remember how they had that big party with all the nudists?"

Everyone laughed, a little too loudly, as if the very thought of nudists was inherently hilarious.

When the braying died down, Jen looked expectantly at Dad, who cleared his throat. "They weren't actually nudists, Geena, they just liked—"

"To take off their clothes," Mom interjected.

"And remember how I ate like three pot brownies?"

Suddenly the mild chuckles dive-bombed into dead silence.

"You ate *marijuana*?" Jen asked, her smile going twitchy, her glance darting to Mom. "When you were *eight*?"

Mom smoothed her hair. "She didn't really—"

"Not on purpose or anything," I clarified. "There was just this plate of brownies on the coffee table and I was like, 'Hey, those look yummy!' The next thing I knew I was walking around the house going, 'I'm dreaming, Mommy! I'm dreaming!'"

"They were very mild," Dad said, frowning. "She—it was nothing."

Mom's grin looked painful. "Dan was supposed to be watching her. Guess that's what happens when you assume Daddy's in charge."

Jen and Mungo both swiveled around to glare at Dad like he'd sprouted horns.

"Oh, if I recall correctly, *I* was supposed to watch her because *you* couldn't take your eyes off that guitarist—what was his name? Something asinine, Woody or Wolfgang—"

"Wyatt. His name was Wyatt."

"Riiiiight." Dad nodded, then looked toward the ceiling as if Wyatt's face were floating there. "Wyatt the Mick Jagger wannabe."

How had this gone so horribly askew? In my mind it was

an amusing, fluffy little anecdote to fill up the blank space where normal conversation should have been. Suddenly, we were waltzing down Bad Memory Lane.

The doorbell rang, and I sprang from my seat. "I'll get it!" I didn't care if it was a Jehovah's Witness working overtime; I had to escape the messy avalanche I'd started.

It was Ben. He had on a gray hat and a wool sweater with his messenger bag slung over his shoulder. His cheeks were rosy from the cold and his dark eyes sparkled in the dim porch light. I'd never been so happy to see anyone in my life.

"Oh, my God," I said, pulling him inside. "You're psychic. Did you pick up on my SOS?"

"What is it? Family trouble?"

"Totally! Why me? Come in here a second, help me get out of this."

We went into the dining room, where each of the adults treated Ben to their own unique brand of Christmas cheer: Mom fawned, Dad glowered, Mungo joked, and Jen flirted. I endured this to the best of my ability, announced we'd be in my room with an innocence that implied we planned to play Chinese checkers there, grabbed Ben's hand, and disappeared before anyone could argue.

Ben's been in my room on exactly two other occasions during the five months we've been dating. Most of our time together has been spent in public places: school, the movies, football games, that sort of thing. The few times we've been alone in my room, things have gotten a little . . . sweaty. It was exhilarating, but also slightly terrifying. The further we got, the more I felt this weird vertigo, you know, like climbing higher and higher until you're scared to look down, but all the same you can feel the yawning drop below and it makes you dizzy.

As much as I like Ben, I'm not totally sure about going all the way. Maybe it's the STD warnings Mom's been feeding me since I was old enough to shave. Maybe it's just that having sex for the first time is a really big deal. It's not like I was raised with fear of hell or anything—I don't believe God takes an active interest in my hymen—it's just that the first time is so . . . irreversible. Whenever I try to picture it with Ben, I just feel overwhelmingly naked. Okay, obviously *naked*, yes, but what I mean is *naked* naked. Like sometimes, right before he kisses me, he stares so deeply into my eyes, I'm afraid he can see every last secret, right down to the most perverted micro-thought that ever flashed through the very back of my mind. It's kind of how I imagine Lois Lane feels when Superman looks at her with his X-ray eyes.

"Why are they *doing* that?" Ben asked as he shrugged off his messenger bag and sat down on my bed.

"What?"

"Your parents. Why are they having dinner with their . . . dates?"

I shook my head. "God only knows. The elderly live in a world of their own."

"Come here." He held out a hand. I slipped my fingers inside his and let him pull me toward him.

Next thing I knew I was in his lap, breathing in his damp wool smell. He looked into my eyes and our lips touched—just barely at first. Then he cupped the back of my head and pulled me closer, deepening the kiss. I flattened my palm against his cheek and the cold of his skin contrasted nicely with the hot, wet interior of his mouth.

We sank back against the bed, breathing faster now. God, things sure do accelerate rapidly when we're alone. It's probably a good thing we've only been in my room a couple of times; give us a bed and a little privacy, we're suddenly on a freight train racing straight for Devirginization City.

Am I unnaturally obsessed with my own virginity? It's not like I intend to wait until marriage or anything. I just want to be sure. Is that so wrong? Sure about what, exactly, I don't know. Will the clouds part as a ray of sunlight illuminates the divine being meant to be my first? I doubt it.

"You okay?" Ben pulled away slightly and studied me.

"Yeah. Why?"

"You just look sort of . . . worried, is all."

I propped myself up on one elbow and shook my head. "No. I'm good."

"You're wondering what I got you, huh?" He flashed a mischievous grin.

"For Christmas?"

"No, for Easter! Yes, for Christmas."

"Well, now that you mention it, I'm a little curious, sure."

He sat up, dug into his messenger bag, and produced a shiny silver box with a big red velvet bow. I could tell by the size and shape of it he'd gotten me clothing of some sort. That made me nervous right away. I'm just not an easy girl to shop for. I know what I like, but nobody—not my friends or parents, certainly not a *guy*—has ever been able to crack the mysterious code of my taste. Clothing is especially nerve-racking, because even if I fake enthusiasm, the giver knows pretty quickly that they missed the mark when I bury said item in the darkest corner of my closet.

"Go on," he said, nudging me, "open it."

My palms began to sweat as I untied the bow. As I lifted the lid off the box, the smell of new clothing wafted up. I peeled back the layers of translucent tissue paper and fished out a filmy red camisole. As I held it up before me, I saw the little black silhouette of a skater chick silk screened onto the breast. She looked like me! Seriously, with braids and everything.

"Oh my God. Did Amber do that?" It had her style written all over it—sort of tattoo-parlor-meets-anime.

"Yeah." He grinned. "She designed it for me. You like?"

"How could I not?"

"But wait." His eyes sparkled with impish glee. "There's more."

I dug a little deeper into the folds of tissue paper and pulled out matching panties. The style was sort of . . . what do you call it? Brazilian? I mean, it wasn't a thong, but it was way more skimpy and up-your-butt than I usually go for.

"Wow," I croaked.

Ben glanced at my bedroom door. "Maybe you should try them on."

I just looked at him.

He shrugged, all innocence. "I mean, you know, to be sure they fit."

No way was I going to prance around my room like a lingerie model when either of my parental units (or aspiring-units—ack!) could barge in at any second. Even if we were the only ones in the house, I still wouldn't relish the prospect. Not that I'm fat or anything, but I'm also not so proud of my bootie that I'm willing to bare three-quarters of it with the lights on.

"Or not," Ben added, sensing my discomfort.

"Maybe some other time."

"Do you like it, though? I asked Sophie what I should get you, and she said no girl can resist lingerie."

I bristled. "You asked *Sophie?*"

"Uh-huh."

The thought of Ben talking to Sophie about underwear made my stomach feel all sour and my throat feel chalky. What the hell was he doing asking *her? No girl can resist lingerie,* huh? Did I even *like* lingerie? Was something wrong with me?

Ben brushed his knuckles along my jaw. "What's going on, Sloane?"

"Nothing. I was just wondering why you didn't ask Amber. I mean, she designed it, right?"

"She made the decal, but I picked out what to put it on—I mean, Sophie helped me pick it out."

"Did you two go *shopping?*"

He shrugged. "Yeah. It was no big deal."

No big deal?! I wanted to scream. I could feel my head getting ready to explode. Somehow, I kept breathing until the urge to hyperventilate passed. The last thing I wanted was to act like a possessive, insecure, sniveling *girlfriend.* With supreme self-control, I folded the panties, put them back in the box, and wrapped my arms around his neck.

"They're great. Seriously. Thank you so much."

He looked at me sideways. "Yeah? You don't have to say that just to be nice . . ."

"I'm not." I flashed for a second on Ben and Sophie walking hand in hand at the mall, but I stomped on that thought too. "Really."

"Cool. I'm glad you like it."

"Okay, time for your present." I got up, opened my under-wear drawer, and pulled out a smallish box wrapped in blue paper dotted with tiny elves.

"What is it?"

"Hello! Open it and find out."

He pulled the paper off slowly. Inside was a collector's edition of *Frankenstein*, one of his favorite books, and a CD I burned full of songs that make me think of him. I'd made my own label for the CD; it was a picture of us last summer, around the time we first got together. It seemed dangerously cheesy—so much so that I almost chickened out at the last second—but I wanted my gift to be personal, not just a *thing*. Also, I looked pretty hot in the picture, so that countered the cheese factor in a big way.

"Very cool," he said, studying the CD first, then the book. "Awesome. Thank you."

I felt all shy again, suddenly. "You're welcome."

He leaned over and kissed me. Then he kissed me again. And again.

I found myself reaching for him, running my hands through his hair, tasting his lips, and all thoughts of Sophie dissolved. Sort of.

Thursday, January 1
11:15 A.M.

Amber's been forced to celebrate the new year with her mom in Lake County, and Ben went skiing with his parents up at Lake Tahoe. Since Hero's boyfriend, Claudio, lives in Italy and she's not quite obscenely rich enough to charter a plane there on a whim, she and I spent an uneventful holiday at her house watching girlie movies, painting our toenails, and pigging out on the awesome crepes their chef Elodie prepared. Hero's house on Moon Mountain is about twenty times the size of our place and she's got hi-def TV on a massive plasma screen, so obviously we decided to kick it there. Once we'd ODed on crepes and settled in to watch *Step Up 2*, Uncle Leo came in, all dressed up in a gray flannel suit, smelling of expensive aftershave.

"I'm almost out of here. Where did I put my damn keys? Did you get enough to eat? You're not having a party, are you?" He straightened his tie, using the floor-to-ceiling window as a mirror. "I'll keep my phone on, in case anything—"

"Dad, just go!" Hero scolded. "Sharon will be furious if you're late again."

Sharon's the party planner Uncle Leo hired for Hero's disastrous birthday bash last summer. She's not exactly the woman I would pick out for him, but it's cool that he's finally dating. He didn't go out with anyone for ages after Hero's mom died. Since both Hero and Bronwyn are away at school now, leaving Leo to rattle around in his mansion all alone, it's good to know he's got someone to spend time with.

When he'd gone, I asked Hero, "How do you think it's going with them, anyway?"

She looked surprised. "With who?"

"Your dad and Sharon."

Her forehead wrinkled momentarily, then smoothed out again. "Okay, I guess. He says he's out of practice."

"I hope that doesn't mean what it sounds like."

She tossed a pillow at me. "Not with—eugh, I don't even want to think about—" She made a choking sound. "No, with dating. You know, showing up on time, communicating—all those things women expect."

I thought of Dad and Jen, Mom and Mungo, all of them back on the market after decades spent in marriages that unexpectedly just—phhht!—disappeared. How weird it must be to start from scratch, relearn all the old mating rituals in a radically altered world.

"Forget about Dad, I want to hear about you and Ben!" Hero snuggled deeper into the suede couch and hugged her knees. "You two haven't gone all the way yet, have you?"

I rolled my eyes. "Hardly. I would have told you!"

"Well, I figured, but you're so weird about guys."

"How am I weird? I'm not weird."

"Come on! You wouldn't even admit you liked Ben until we tricked you into it."

"Okay," I assented, "that's half-true. But I didn't really know how much I liked him until I realized he liked me."

"So, how is it now? Are you madly in love?"

I thought about it. "I have fun with him. He makes me laugh. I don't know, though, something makes me nervous about this whole couple thing."

She looked confused. "What 'couple thing'?"

"Oh, you know, calling him my 'boyfriend,' going on 'dates,' getting all intense about everything. I mean, he's still Ben, right? I'm still Geena. I'm not crazy about giving up my autonomy so I can blur into this slimy blob of oneness."

She snickered. "'Slimy blob of oneness'? How romantic."

"You know what I mean."

She studied me, then reached over and plucked up one of the Belgian chocolates Elodie had arranged on a glass plate. "You know what it is? You hate feeling out of control."

My instinct was to deny it immediately. I mean, come on, one of my favorite things to do is bomb a hill that's almost too steep to survive. If that's not out of control, I don't know what is.

Before I could protest, though, another thought hit me: Skating is all about control, actually. It's about taking on gravity, using everything you've got to show it who's boss. Otherwise it wouldn't be skating so much as careening wildly on a piece of plywood, plummeting to your death.

"You can't control love." Hero went all annoyingly wise on me like she sometimes does. "*It* controls *you*."

"Okay, Little Miss Love Guru," I told her. "If you say so."

Monday, January 5
9:20 P.M.

Ah, the grind. Winter break is officially kaput, Hero's back at boarding school, and so far the semester looks excruciatingly grim. Classes have reached a new level of torture:

1) First-period PE to ensure I'll be sweaty and red-faced all day. Thank you, sadistic counselors.

2) AP Trig, where my brain will jump out of my skull like a jack-in-the-box every morning, leaving me the rest of the day to cram it back in.

3) AP Chemistry. Just in case there's any brain left to eject.

4) Third-year French. Madame Peck is famous for discussing delicious cuisine from every region, which I'm sure my pre-lunch digestive juices will appreciate.

5) AP History with Ms. Boyle, the civil rights–obsessed Goddess of Flowing Armpit Hair.

6) AP English. With Bricker. Enough said.

Sometimes I suspect AP actually stands for Aggravated Psoriasis—just thinking about that schedule is enough to make me itch all over.

Wednesday, January 7
10:20 P.M.

This afternoon I was walking from fifth-period history to sixth-period English when I heard someone calling my name. Okay, "someone calling my name" is a little bit misleading; I knew right away it was Ben.

The thing is, every day this week he's stopped me between fifth and sixth period, and every time, we've ended up kissing there in the hallway, which is just so totally un-me. I mean sure, kissing Ben is always a peak experience, but in the hallway? The fragrance of multiple generations' body odor and bad cafeteria fries just doesn't really get me in the mood. Also, I'm Geena Sloane, and if I have any identity whatsoever at Sonoma Valley High, it's as a scrappy, slightly boy-hostile skater Betty, meaning I do not make out in the halls like some cheerleader.

So today I did what any self-respecting non-hallway-kisser would do: I ignored him.

Except he didn't get the hint.

"Hey, Sloane! Wait up." He actually reached out and touched my arm.

At that point, I either had to feign a walking-dead-like indifference to human touch, or acknowledge him. I chose the latter. After all, he is basically my boyfriend, right?

"Oh, hey. How's it going?"

He gave me a once-over. "You were really in your own little world there. I called your name like four times. Everything okay?"

"Yeah, I was just—you know—thinking about, um, Malcolm X."

"Malcolm . . . X?"

"American history? Hello, you were there too. Weren't you listening to Ms. Boyle?" Ben and I have almost every class together; it's the blessing and the curse of the AP track. All of us college-bound kids move from one grueling subject to the next, like a pack of lemmings.

He grinned sheepishly. "I was kind of fixated on your braids, actually."

"My braids," I repeated dryly.

"Yeah." He reached out and took one of them in his hand. "This one's got a reddish streak right . . . here."

Okay, that was pretty cute. But if I started getting all goo-goo eyed, we'd end up locking lips again, and the whole point of Operation Ignore Him was to nip this PDA habit in the bud.

"Unless Ms. Boyle suddenly decides to quiz us on the his-

tory of hair, I doubt studying my braids is going to help you
ace the class. And remember, you *do* need an A if you want to
keep up with me."

Ben and I have been vying for top academic ranking since
the fifth grade, and every semester we either tie or leap-frog
ahead of each other by a fraction of a GPA point. Our com-
petition used to be fierce, but since we got together we've
been less openly cutthroat. Lately, I almost miss our boldly
hostile race for valedictorian.

He cupped the back of my neck gently with his hand and
said, "You let me worry about my grades, okay?"

I stiffened. His hand on my neck was totally giving me
goose bumps, but this was the road to get-a-room-style hallway make-out sessions, and I *have* to remember that's not who
I am. Don't I?

I glanced down at my Pumas. "Ben—I—"

But it was too late. As soon as I looked up again, his lips
were closing in on mine, warm and scented with cinnamon.
His other hand found the small of my back, and I could feel
everything in me pulling toward him, my heart racing, my
head filling with his smell.

"Bettaglia shoots—he scores!"

I pulled away, startled, and caught sight of PJ tossing us
a sly smile over his shoulder. Apparently, I have zero self-
control, and will soon be known as SVHS's newest Hallway
Hoochie.

The bell rang, and we headed for English.

"Why do you always kiss me between fifth and sixth?" I
asked.

Ben looked mildly offended. "What do you mean?"

"Well, we've got like four other classes together. Why is it always before this one that you decide to molest me?" I tried to infuse *molest* with the perfect mixture of playfulness and *Heads-up: I'm not a PDA ho,* but I don't think he picked up on my artful subtext.

"In history, I sit right behind you. Listening to tales of bloodshed and disaster while staring at the back of your neck *inspires* me, I guess."

Okay, that was also a little cute. Bettaglia two, Sloane zero.

○ ● ● ○ ● ○

Our English teacher, Mrs. Bricker, wasn't slumped at her desk like she usually is, carving red slashes into a stack of papers. In fact, she wasn't anywhere in sight.

Oooohh, maybe she died, I thought, and I'll admit the idea pleased me. Mrs. Bricker is four hundred years old, give or take a century, with hairy moles, crumpled Kleenex that rain from her pockets, and a tendency to break into hour-long soliloquies about the uses and abuses of the semicolon. Her nickname at SVHS is Mobydiculous, referring simultaneously to her pathological obsession with Herman Melville and her famously unrealistic insistence on twenty-page theme papers.

English is my best subject, but try as I might, I just can't get stoked about some creepy dude's love affair with a massive white whale. If only Melville's editor had used a red pen as liberally on *his* early drafts as Mrs. Bricker does on ours.

Since Ben's last name is Bettaglia and mine's Sloane, we have to sit at opposite ends of the room in all of our classes with assigned seats. Most of the teachers at SVHS cling to this outdated pedagogy—heaven forbid we should sit near someone we have more in common with than our placement in the alphabet. Unfortunately, this fascist practice makes Ben a sitting duck for none other than Sophie De Luca, who draped herself over Ben's desk the second he sat down. I hovered nearby, sneaking glances at them while I pretended to sharpen my pencil.

"What's up, Benedict?"

Why does she get away with that? He hates his full name, but it never seems to bother him when *she* says it.

"Nothing. What about you?"

"Same old."

I guess this conversation sounds pretty benign, but even from my pencil sharpening station I could see she was using her glamorous insouciance to ensnare him in her web. She looked fabu as usual. She had on a suede tam-o'-shanter, a silk tunic, fashionably distressed jeans, and these high-heeled boots that I just know cost more than the sum total of my college fund. How does she get up every morning and *do* that—just throw on an outfit of unsurpassed style and intolerable *je ne sais quois?* I'd pay good money to see her in ratty sweats and a drool-stained sweatshirt. The depressing thing is, she'd probably manage to look fabulous even in that.

"Moby's MIA," Sophie observed, nodding at the empty desk at the front of the room.

That's another thing about Sophie: She's been at SVHS less than a week, and you'd think she'd been here forever. She's got this uncanny ability to assess the social landscape, memorize its topography, and magically instill herself as ruling monarch before anyone has time to blink.

Luckily, Principal Hardbaugh shuffled in right then, distracting me from my urge to puke all over my beautiful, charismatic rival.

"Okay, everyone in your seats, I've got some news."

We all flew to our desks. A low murmur filled the room, but it ceased when Hardbaugh frowned at us and held up a hand. The wrinkles in his forehead formed ridges that spread from his furrowed brows all the way up to the smooth dome of his bald head. His unwieldy, gray plastic glasses and puke-colored polyester suit were probably cool. In 1973.

"I'm sorry to say I've got sad news. Mrs. Bricker slipped in the shower last night and broke her hip. Fortunately, we were able to secure a long-term substitute at short notice. In fact, Dr. Rex Sands should be here any moment." He glanced at his watch and tugged at his collar. I couldn't help thinking, *Moby gives this place the best centuries of her life, and it takes them five minutes to replace her.*

"Excuse me, Mr. Hardbaugh?" Before I knew what I was doing, my hand was in the air and Mr. H was swiveling his furrowed brow in my direction.

"Yes, Geena?"

"Don't you think a day of mourning would be appropriate? I mean, Mrs. Bricker's not well. We're naturally a little shaken." I looked around at my AP comrades. "We could probably all use a little time to ourselves."

Everyone saw where I was headed with this and immediately nodded in assent, doing their best to look stricken with grief. Unfortunately, Hardbaugh also saw right through my suggestion. He pushed his unfortunate glasses up onto the bridge of his nose and squinted at me.

"Young lady, the broken hip of Mrs. Bricker should not be viewed as an opportunity to cruise in your souped-up cars or smoke *Mary Jane*." He reached again for his collar and gave it an irritated yank. "Frankly, the fact that you'd try to manipulate the situation at a time like this is very disappointing, Ms. Sloane."

For a second, I actually did feel a stab of guilt, not to mention a flash of concern that Hardbaugh could somehow sabotage my much-anticipated free ride to Yale. Both were fleeting, though, because right then an exceptionally well-built, broad-shouldered, babelicious twentysomething guy dashed into the room wearing a tweed blazer and faded Levi's.

"Sorry I'm late," he breathed. His hair was short and dark blond, his eyes a moody gray.

"Take your seat, young man." Mr. H indicated an empty desk with a curt nod.

The hottie hid a grin, stuck out his hand, and said in a deep, self-consciously professional voice, "Actually, I'm Rex Sands, sir."

Mr. Hardbaugh didn't seem to understand for a moment. He merely blinked at the fabulous specimen before him.

"This is room twenty-three, right? Aren't you expecting a sub?"

Hardbaugh snapped out of the geriatric spell he'd lapsed into. "Mr. Sands? *Dr.* Sands?"

The guy nodded. In one rapid movement he pulled his cell from his pocket, stealthily checked the display, and turned it off. "At your service. I hit traffic on the way up—my apologies."

When Mr. H finally realized he had an actual *person* before him—not the subhuman teen variety, but a bona fide adult—his whole demeanor switched instantly from condescending to sycophantic. It was a terrifying transformation. "Dr. Sands, I can't tell you how happy we are to have you on board."

"Oh, thanks." Sands turned to us briefly, and maybe it was wishful thinking, but the look on his face seemed to say, *I'll get rid of this fossil, just give me a second.*

Mr. H continued to size up hottielicious as he said, "Class, this is Dr. Sands, your sub for the rest of the school year."

Every female in the room sucked in her breath, which triggered a barely audible grumble of disgust from the males.

"Technically, sir, I'm not really a doctor until I—"

"Dr. Sands has just finished his PhD in English Literature at UC Berkeley, and is currently writing his dissertation on . . . ?"

Dr. Hottie stuffed both hands into his pockets and said, "Kerouac and the beat poets—Ginsburg, Snyder, those guys."

Mr. H flashed him the peace sign. "Hip cats."

"Uh . . . yeah."

"Excellent. Well, I'll leave you to it, then. Drop by my office as soon as you're done, and we'll go over your contract."

As Mr. H finally exited, Dr. Hottie turned to us. He really was beyond gorgeous. He was tall, with the long, ropy muscles of a runner. The gray eyes hinted at brooding intensity and probing intelligence. I felt my heart hammering wildly inside me.

"So, I guess this is a pretty weird day for you guys. You just heard about Mrs. Bricker?"

We nodded in unison, entranced. All thoughts of Mrs. Bricker had evaporated.

"You're juniors, right?" He pulled a folder from his bat-
tered leather messenger bag and leaned against the desk, flipping through pages. "Oh, right, AP English. Cool, so you're
the smart ones."

We were too smart to agree to that; instead, we gazed at
him in silence.

"Look, I'll be honest with you." He ran one hand over his
head and the hair sprang up from beneath his palm at odd
angles, making him somehow even more adorable. "I never
wanted to teach high school—still don't—but Mrs. Bricker
was a friend of my mom's, and I've got to get out of Berkeley
for a while so I can stop partying and bang out this damn dissertation. Oh, shit, can I say damn in here?"

We burst out laughing. Well, the girls did, anyway. The
guys, you could tell, were playing hard to get, trying to decide
whether to idolize or resent him. Ben shot me a quick look
over his shoulder and I bit my lip, suddenly recalling that I
have a boyfriend now and shouldn't be lusting over Dr. Hottie,
especially when said boyfriend is just five rows away.

"So, what are you guys reading, again?"

"*Moby-Dick*," we grumbled.

"Melville." He spit it out like the two syllables pained him.
"Fine, okay, that's cool. How far in are you?"

I raised my hand and he nodded at me. God, he was cute.
"We were supposed to finish chapter five by tomorrow. If you
ask me, though, putting this book on the syllabus is part of a
terrorist plot to make Americans hate literature."

He smiled. "What's your name?"

I could feel everyone staring at me, and my cheeks went
hot. "Geena Sloane."

"You know what, Geena Sloane? I couldn't agree with you more." He started pulling books from his leather bag, all of them tattered and dog-eared. "Look, guys, I've got certain rules I've got to follow—standard curriculum blah-blah-blah—but if it was up to me, we'd start with this book right here." He held up a paperback and I squinted, trying to read the title. "*On the Road*. How many of you have read it?"

Nobody raised a hand.

Mr. Sands clutched at his chest as if he'd been shot. "Get out! Really? Nobody? Tragic! It's an electric, frenzied ode to restless youth. There's a guy in it, Dean Moriarty? Think of the craziest friend you ever had, now multiply that by a hundred. Moriarty's based on this real-life dude, Neal Cassidy . . ."

Mr. Sands went on like that for the rest of the period, his eyes burning with excitement, reeling us in with the dynamic cadence of his velvet voice. I'd heard of the beats before, and this Kerouac guy sounded familiar, but Mr. Sands made me feel like I'd never understand anything about America or freedom or sex or art or holiness until I'd memorized every last syllable of *On the Road*.

I made up my mind to get it from the library first thing.

Friday, January 9
11:40 P.M.

Amber and I were working the evening shift at Triple Shot Betty's when a cute little navy blue MG drove up, sputtering exhaust. The mysterious driver in aviator glasses was none other than Mr. Sands; I beat Amber to the window and took his order.

After asking for a double latte with extra foam, he lowered his glasses and squinted at me. The January light was dazzling, and I noticed for the first time that his smoky eyes had flecks of gold in them.

"Hey, aren't you in my class?"

I grinned shyly. "Yeah."

"What's your name again?"

"Geena Sloane."

"Right, right, Geena. You're the one who called Melville a terrorist plot." He chuckled.

"That's me." I was flattered that he remembered something I'd said, even if it wasn't my finest one-liner. English is my place to shine—the one area in life where I consistently kick ass—and I get really into discussions. Around Mr. Sands, though, I'm a little inhibited. His sheer hunkyosity makes me a nervous wreck.

As I brewed Mr. Sands's latte, Amber took advantage of the vacated window space and leaned onto her elbows, providing him with a tempting view of her freckled cleavage. "So *you're* the legendary Mr. Sands."

I glanced over just in time to see his Adam's apple jerk in response. "Guilty. And you are . . . ?"

"Amber."

"Amber. Nice. I like color names."

She let out a throaty laugh. "I'm pretty colorful."

"So, what does 'legendary' mean, exactly?"

"Oh, come on," she teased, "you're the English teacher— you tell me!" She peeked out from under her lashes and added in a husky voice, "You must have a huge . . . vocabulary."

Um, can anyone say Over the top?

"You're not in any of my classes, are you?"

Was it my imagination, or did his voice just crack?

"No. . . ." She paused, not meeting his eyes.

Mr. Sands only teaches AP English. Despite Amber's apparent aspirations as most creative flirt, she barely pulls C's in basic English, so AP isn't an option.

I caught a glimpse of her profile and I knew, with a sudden flash of dread, that she'd stumbled on an idea. When Amber gets an idea, look out.

"Actually, I'm a college student."

I was just delivering his latte and was so caught off guard by the lie that I sucked in too much air, inducing a dramatic coughing fit. Horrified, I hastily deposited the drink at the window and shrank into the shadows, practically hyperventilating. I didn't want Mr. Sands to worry I'd spray spittle all over his mounds of creamy foam.

"Thanks, Geena," he called. "Looks perfect."

I smiled weakly. *Don't mind me, I'm just the spastic espresso wench.*

Amber rang him up, though how she could operate the register and shoot such flirty glances simultaneously was a mystery to me. While handing him his change, she cooed, "Would you like our Betty Bargain Card? If you come see us twelve times, the thirteenth will be our treat." Somehow she managed to infuse the word *treat* with pornographic undertones.

"Don't mind if I do, actually."

It was hard to be sure from where I stood, but it looked like Mr. Sands was blushing.

As he drove away, Amber lingered at the window, craning her neck to watch until he hung a left and disappeared.

"Oh my God," she breathed. "I'm in love."

This might not seem like a newsflash coming from most girls, but from the mouth of Amber it was shocking. She's always insisted boys are like bad TV: entertaining if you've got nothing better to do, downright pathetic if examined too closely. The one time she did fall for a guy, he betrayed her so brutally, I don't blame her for becoming an anti-love evangelist. Now she was spinning slowly away from the window, her upturned face full of dreamy innocence, like an ingénue in some cheesy musical about to break into song.

"Who are you and what did you do with my friend Amber?"

She looked at me like she'd completely forgotten I was there. When memory of my existence fully registered, her eyes went wide and she addressed me in a tone of reverence. "You have English with him, don't you?"

"Yeah . . ."

"Thank God, thank God, thank God!"

"Wait a minute—I don't like the sound of this . . ."

She seized my hands. "You have to help me! I need to know everything there is to know about him."

"Because . . . ?"

She blew her hair out of her eyes, exasperated. "Duh! I'm totally into him! You need to do reconnaissance so I can win him."

"*Win* him? You're kidding, right?"

"Of course not."

I made a face. "He's way out of your league."

She looked so hurt, I had to backpedal.

"No—I mean, not—I don't mean it that way, it's just—come on, Amber, he's a *teacher*. It's like . . . illegal."

"You're telling me a high school teacher can't date a college girl?"

I blinked. "Well, maybe when you're in college . . ."

She grinned wickedly. "Didn't you hear me? I *am* in college."

"Ah-hah. . . ."

"Except I'll need your help."

I took a step back. "I don't know."

"Don't worry; it'll be easy. Just be my eyes and ears. You spend an hour with him five days a week—"

"Fifty minutes."

She ignored my interruption. "That gives you plenty of time to find out everything about him."

I rolled my eyes. "Yeah, I can just see it: 'Mr. Sands, when's our Melville quiz? Oh, and while you're at it, can you describe your ideal date?'"

"What's Melville?"

I sighed. "Even if we do manage to convince him you're in college, if he spots you at school, we're busted."

"Don't you worry about that." Her face was sly, calculating various scenarios like a general planning an ambush. "All you have to concentrate on right now is information gathering."

Monday, January 12
8:00 P.M.

Was just putting the final touches on my French homework when I heard the doorbell. Since she said she might stop by, I figured it was Amber. I danced dramatically to the door, singing in a loud, fakey operatic baritone, scraping together scraps of French that made *absolument* no sense together. *"Vous avez déjà vu c'est la vie sacre bleu! Fermez la booooouuuuuu—"* I held the note and flung open the door.

It was Ben.

The climactic scene in my Opera of the Mind fizzled abruptly as I clamped my mouth shut and blushed.

"Hi." He shoved one hand into the pocket of his jeans and ran the other over his dark hair. I could see he was hiding a smile. "You, uh, rehearsing?"

"Oh, just, you know"—I tapped my chest—"warming up the old pipes."

"Didn't know you were a baritone." The smile was winning now, cracking open in spite of his efforts to squelch it. "I would've pegged you as an alto."

I lifted my chin a little. "I'm versatile. What's up?"

I knew my tone was too brusque when his expression went suddenly neutral. "Uh, nothing, really, just thought I'd stop by."

See, this is just way too confusing. I'm always psyched to see Ben, but never knowing when he'll show up infringes on my freedom to be weird-beyond-reason in the privacy of my own home. Is that even healthy? I have to watch myself all day at school, guarding my image, and now I have to be self-conscious after hours too?

"If it's a bad time . . ." he began.

I shook my head. "No, I'm sorry, come on in."

He stepped inside.

"Um, you want a soda or something?" I headed toward the kitchen.

"Sure—or maybe just water?"

"Water, water everywhere and not a drop to drink!" I don't know why I said that. *Why did I say that?* I busied my hands pouring myself some ginger ale and him a glass of water from the filter. We've never been completely alone here before—there's always been an adult lurking somewhere. Now Mom was out with Mungo and wouldn't be back for hours.

"I went for a great ride today. Took Arnold Drive over to Sonoma Mountain. It's beautiful up there."

Ben's a cyclist—he's pretty serious about it. I think he clocks like four thousand miles a week or something. I know nothing about bikes.

"Cool," was all I could think of to say.

The kitchen clock ticked away methodically. The refrigerator hummed. He took a step toward me and our noses were mere centimeters apart. I could feel his breath on my face. We just stayed there for a long moment, the electricity between us surging and crackling with alarming intensity.

"What's going on with you, Sloane?" His lips grazed mine as he murmured the question.

Every synapse in my body started firing off X-rated messages. Glands and organs I didn't even know I possessed were throbbing in time with his all-too-audible breathing.

"Nothing," I mumbled weakly.

"What is it? Am I coming on too strong?" He pressed his nose ever so lightly along my jaw, and then his breath caressed the inside of my ear. I looked down and saw goose bumps spreading from my shoulder to my wrist like an ocean turning to whitecaps under a steady breeze.

I wonder what my ear looks like that close up. Is it delicate and conch-like, or are we talking scary little tarantula hairs? Brain, please shut up now.

"Well, am I?" he asked.

I'd lost track of the conversation. "Are you what?"

"Am I coming on too strong?"

"No." I hope he didn't notice my voice cracking.

When his lips finally found mine, I felt myself start to relax and sink into it. There was no need to get all wiggy—this was Ben, my friend, my rival, and okay, yes, my boyfriend. It wasn't like he was going to push me into having sex with him before I knew what I wanted. I thought of Hero's observation: *You despise feeling out of control.* Maybe I just needed to stop trying to control this thing between us. Maybe then I could stop being so weird.

Without warning, I felt his hand slip under my shirt and cup my breast. I flinched. It just seemed so abrupt this time, without the usual slow-paced prelude. The cadence of our kissing changed—it became more urgent, less playful—and all at once I felt like I was being swallowed.

I leaned away from him. "Uh . . ."

His hand didn't move. It formed an odd, lumpy mass under my shirt. I looked down at it, and so did he.

"What's wrong?" he asked.

"I just—I don't know. You startled me."

He stared into my eyes, and his expression was so intense, so hungry, he almost didn't look like Ben. "Geena, I'm really into you. You know that, right?"

I may not be all that schooled in sexual matters, but I could feel pretty clear evidence of that pressing against me. "Um . . . yeah. I'm into you too."

His hand slipped under my bra and he leaned in to kiss my neck. Okay, this was getting a little intense. And that felt good. Really good. Inside my head I was like, *Is this happening?* Am I going to lose my virginity right here, in my mother's kitchen, next to the microwave? Shouldn't we be—I don't know—*closer* than this? Shouldn't I know everything about him—not just his middle name or his GPA, but his darkest secrets too? Shouldn't he know *me* better? Because what if we do this and *then* he gets to know me better and realizes I'm not all that brilliant, I just study harder than most people, and I have a weird mole sprouting hair on my left thigh and pineapple gives me gas? We haven't even used the L-word yet. Tomorrow morning, when I walk into trig and see him sitting there, talking to Sophie De Luca, will I feel all va-va-voom, or will I freak out that I gave away some crucial part of myself and now I can't get it back?

"Knock, knock!"

We jerked away from each other, startled, and turned to see Amber doing an about-face in the kitchen doorway.

"Oops," she said. "Sorry! Didn't mean to interrupt. Everybody decent now?"

I straightened my shirt. "Yeah, everybody's decent."

She turned back around and leaned against the counter. "Whattup, disgustingly happy little lovebirds?"

Ben turned away from her and quickly performed some sort of crotch-adjustment. A part of me was bummed about the interruption, but a bigger part was relieved.

Ben made some excuse about trig homework and hightailed it out of there. When he'd left, Amber crossed her arms over her chest and looked at me, one eyebrow quirked in a question.

"What?" I was instantly defensive.

"Last summer you acted like boys had cooties. Now look at you!"

I groaned, thrusting my hands into my hair. "I don't know what I'm doing! It's so confusing . . ."

"Looks like you're figuring it out."

"I mean, how are you supposed to know when you're ready?" I started chewing on the end of my braid. I can't help myself; it's a nervous tic.

"Oh, come on." Amber's tone implied I was being dense. "You two are madly in love. He's totally cute. What's there to figure out? Are you going to get on the Pill? You should use a condom, even so. Not that Ben's diseased or anything, but still—"

"Amber!" I bugged my eyes at her. "We haven't even said *I love you*. I'm a little freaked out here. Can you slow down, please?"

She hopped onto the counter. "Okay, lay it on me, babe. What's freaking you out?"

I paced the kitchen. "What if we do have sex? Then what?"

"I don't understand the question . . ."

"Come on! How many people in high school stay together for more than a year?"

Her brow furrowed. "I'm not saying you should *marry* him . . ."

"I know, but say we have sex and then we figure out we're not that into each other, so we break up. Think of how much harder that'll be!"

"You're not that into him?"

"I am into him, but . . . say he gets a glimpse of the real me and runs screaming?"

Amber looked incredulous. "Are you kidding? You're the bomb! He'd be an idiot if he—"

"Or what if we have sex and he loses interest because the mystery's gone? Guys do that."

She considered this carefully. "I don't think that's his style. He respects you."

"Even if we have sex and stay together, then what? Who wants to be with their high school sweetheart forever? Isn't that small-town loser-ish?" I felt my spirits plummeting. I thought of my mom and dad, Leo and Aunt Kathy, all of them thinking they'd be together forever back in the day. Now look at them. Aunt Kathy's dead, so she got off the hook, but Mom and Dad and Leo are all just stumbling around in the dark, grasping for something solid and finding only air. "Relationships are doomed, any way you look at it. We're in for a world of pain—it's like Russian roulette!"

"Jeez." Amber sighed. "And you say I'm cynical."

Wednesday, January 14

1:30 P.M.

In history class right now, scribbling in the dark. Ms. Boyle looks like she got run over by a truck—or, more likely, sucked down a few too many G & Ts last night. She popped in some

PBS video about Martin Luther King and is now slipping into a coma behind her desk, so I don't think she'll mind if I write about what happened today at lunch.

Ben, Amber, PJ, and I were kicking it on the grass, soaking up the freakishly warm midwinter rays. Nearby, the stofers were entertaining a small crowd of acne-riddled sophomores, Dog and George challenging each other to consume various disgusting concoctions while Virg caught it all on film. Luckily, I'd already finished my sandwich; otherwise, the sight of Dog eating a live beetle smothered in catsup might have forced my PB & J into a repeat performance.

I was stretched out on my stomach reading chapter thirteen of *On the Road*. I wanted to be totally into it, but the truth is, I had to make myself keep reading. I kept looking for the radiant, electrifying prose Mr. Sands always goes on about, but to me it just felt like one long, queasy car ride with no particular destination.

PJ was telling Ben about some *quinceñera* he DJed last weekend and Amber was listening to her iPod, lounging lazily on her back with her sweatshirt balled up under her head as a makeshift pillow, huge sunglasses covering most of her face. I was getting to the part where Sal Paradise hooks up with this Mexican woman he met on a bus, when Ben came over and lay down straight across from me, his face suddenly inches from mine.

"What are you reading?"

I flipped it over so he could see the cover.

"I guess Mr. Sands dictates your reading list now?"

"It's not that good." I decided to sidestep the topic of Mr. Sands. "I don't quite get why it's such a classic."

Ben nodded. He opened his mouth to say something, but stopped.

"What?" I laughed. "Say it."

"No, I just . . ." He hesitated again, then plowed ahead. "What do you think of Mr. Sands, anyway?"

I glanced over at Amber quickly, but she was lost in the Land of iPod. I didn't really know how to answer Ben. I could hardly say I found our English teacher unspeakably hot, could I? On the other hand, should I out-and-out lie just to save his feelings? I decided to take the path of least resistance: understatement.

"He's cool."

Ben flashed me a disturbingly knowing grin.

"What?" I demanded.

"Nothing. It's just that sometimes, when you say so little, your face says so much."

I sat up, pushing the book aside. "What's that supposed to mean?"

"Don't be mad! Just don't ever go into politics or poker."

"Ha-ha," I said dryly.

PJ tore himself away from the sight of George chewing something majorly repulsive—an earthworm, I think. "You two having a little tiff?"

We both answered simultaneously—I said no and Ben said yes. He was still grinning, though.

"What's the matter, Ben? She reverting to her man-hating ways?"

I snorted. "I'm not a man-hater, okay? I never was."

"No, you're no hater," Ben teased. "I think Mr. Sands has transformed you."

Amber yanked her earbuds out and popped up onto her elbows. "What are you guys talking about?"

"Mr. Sands," PJ grumbled. "Man, that guy's making it hard on the rest of us."

Ben was still looking at me in that I-know-all-your-secrets way. It made me incredibly nervous. Why can't I be like Sophie De Luca—artful and mysterious—instead of walking around exposed all the time, like a great big plucked chicken?

"Mr. Sands," Amber said, "will soon be off the market, so don't even stress."

"Don't tell Geena that." Ben's eyes twinkled. "You'll break her heart."

Amber flopped back down on her makeshift pillow. "Yeah, right. As if G ever looks at anyone besides you."

Ben leaned over and kissed me then—gently, teasingly. As usual, it stirred in me a powerful mixture of self-consciousness and white-hot lust.

"Okay, okay," PJ complained. "Get a room."

Ben's lips murmured against my jaw, "Don't ditch me for Dr. Hipster."

That made me laugh. I pushed him away and shoved Kerouac into my bag. "Don't worry. The only thing I want from 'Dr. Hipster' is an A."

Inside, though, I couldn't help but wonder if Ben already knew more than he should.

Saturday, January 17

11:45 P.M.

This afternoon was the grand opening for Floating World Tattoo. Amber's got a job there a couple afternoons a week, which luckily won't eclipse her other calling, slinging coffee with me at TSB. Her plans for world domination involve branding the youth of America with manga-inspired nymphs, gargoyles, fairies, and other fantastic confections of the mind. I don't really get it, but she's wanted to be a tattoo artist since she was eight or something, so it's good she can apprentice there. At least she knows what she wants—that's way more than I can say.

When we were getting ready, she took one look at my Dickies, T-shirt, and hoodie, then rolled her eyes.

"G, are you wearing that?"

I looked down at my outfit. "Yeah, why?"

Without answering, she started flipping through my closet until she found a low-cut, long-sleeved deep red shirt Jen got me for my birthday. I'd never even put it on.

"Try this!" she ordered.

I did, but reluctantly.

"That looks better. You need a different bra, though." She frowned at the way my tatty old sports bra peeked out from beneath the U-shaped neckline. Digging through her bag, she produced a black lace push-up bra, lightly padded. So convenient, sharing the same bra size with your best friend. Obediently, I took everything off, strapped the Uniboob into this much sexier holster, and pulled the shirt back over my head. She studied the new me with an appraising eye.

"Uh-huh . . ." she muttered, before whipping out a tube of berry red lip gloss and smearing it across my lips.

"Am I acceptable now?" I grumbled sarcastically.

"Much improved. You've got a rival in town. You better start working it."

"A rival? What does that mean?"

She scoffed, leaning toward the mirror to examine her eyeliner. "Don't pretend you haven't noticed."

"Noticed what?"

"Everyone knows Sophie De Luca's after Ben."

I swallowed. When she noticed my silent horror, she spun around and tugged on one of my braids. "Not that he's tempted. Still, it can't hurt to—you know—turn on your love light."

I wondered what that meant. Was my "love light" a padded bra and lip gloss, or was it something more involved—some secret weapon other girls had that I didn't even know about?

Ben picked us up around noon. His eyes registered something when I climbed into the Volvo—surprise, I guess, to see me sans-hoodie—but he didn't say anything, and I wasn't about to fish for compliments.

Walking into Floating World, I felt a twinge of self-consciousness, of not-fitting-in-ness. The space is super cool. It's got exposed steel girders and brick walls—very urban and chic in that pseudo-industrial, Soho loft sort of way. Since the owner, Alistair Drake, used to be the drummer for Stalin's Love Child and his tattoo parlors are considered la bombe, the place was packed with twentysomethings who looked like they'd just stepped out of an AFI video. Everyone had greasy hair streaked with tropical colors, exotic piercings, bared midriffs, and heroin addict bodies. They walked around in a state of glamorous decay, insouciant and grimy as French movie stars. Even in my cleavage-bearing shirt, next to these pale, sylph-like creatures I felt like a chubby, pink-cheeked Girl Scout.

There was a band playing on a small wooden platform. A girl with a shaved head sang and a lanky redhead played bass. The drummer had a scruffy Mohawk. The guitar player looked considerably younger than his band mates, and I thought I recognized him from school. While Amber, Ben, and I hovered around the food table chowing down, guitar guy followed Amber everywhere with his eyes, as if there were invisible wires connecting his pupils to her face.

"I think lead guitar likes you," I teased.

She glanced over her shoulder at him and scoffed. "Jeremy? Yeah, like that'd work."

"Why? What's wrong with him?"

"Oh, come on, G, he's a total emo-kid."

Ben tilted his head appraisingly. "He's got a kick-ass Strat."

Amber rolled her eyes at Ben while I studied the boy in question more carefully. He was pale, with the milky, pure complexion of a British schoolboy. His black hair was streaked with indigo; it cascaded over his forehead and concealed much of his face. When he shook it aside, you could see that his eyes were gorgeous—strikingly blue, sapphire-bright. Though I'd never really noticed him before, he was intriguing, in an art-boy sort of way. In fact, he looked a little like one of Amber's sketches . . . indie-cool, slightly androgynous, with manga-style eyes that made the rest of his face blur into the background.

"Have you ever talked to him?" I asked Amber.

She blew her hair out of her eyes impatiently. "Yeah. Here and there."

"And . . . ?"

"And nothing . . . He looks twelve!" Unfortunately, the music stopped just before she spit out this last part, and her voice was loud enough for everyone to hear. A couple trendy girls in tiny T-shirts giggled. Jeremy dropped his eyes to his guitar, looking dejected.

The band took a break then, most of them sauntering toward the exit. Jeremy didn't follow, though. Instead he leaned against the far wall, hands in his pockets, trying hard not to look at Amber, but failing miserably. I felt bad for him. I caught his eye and tried to convey a welcoming, *we won't bite* vibe. Finally he pushed away from the wall and walked over to us.

"Hey," he said, peeking up at Amber through his hair. "How's it going?"

Amber looked bored. "Just groovy. You?"

"Yeah, fine."

"I'm Geena," I said. "This is Ben. Love your band. What are you guys called?"

"The Aqua Nets."

I grinned. "Cool."

"We've got some good gigs coming up." His eyes darted to Amber, then over to Ben and back to me. "We're playing the

Raven Theater in a couple weeks." When Amber didn't even look at him, he added, "Probably start around eight."

An awkward pause ensued. Amber glanced from one corner of the room to another, while Jeremy studied his scuffed Doc Martens.

"Maybe we'll go!" I blurted. What was wrong with Amber? Why couldn't she give the kid a break?

"That'd be cool."

I stepped subtly on Amber's toe. "Wouldn't that be fun? I've never been to the Raven."

She just mumbled a noncommittal "Maybe."

Then all at once Amber's face lit up. Her cheeks flushed, she licked her lips, and her eyes abandoned their dull glaze for a sparkly, expectant glow.

I looked over my shoulder and spotted Mr. Sands squinting in through the plate-glass windows. He had a slight case of bed-head, and his usual five o'clock shadow had thickened to something a shade darker. He was wearing a threadbare T-shirt that might have been yellow years ago, but had long since faded to dishwater-gray. His ancient Levi's hung low on his hips, revealing just the waistband of his boxer shorts.

"Oh my God," Amber breathed. "He's here."

Jeremy looked perplexed. "Mr. Sands? You have him for English?"

Ben rolled his eyes. "Great. Doctor Hipster to the rescue."

"Catch you guys later." Amber walked away from us abruptly, and I thought for a second she'd go talk to him. Even Amber didn't have enough nerve to approach Mr. Sands directly, though. Instead she hovered at the edge of the window, peeking out with besotted puppy dog eyes until the object of her affection wandered off down the street. Only then did she dare go outside to the sidewalk and stare after him wistfully.

Jeremy didn't look well. His already pale complexion had turned skim-milk white. I'd never talked to him before today, but seeing his cheeks drained of color like that, my heart went out to the poor kid.

"She's got a little crush, but I don't see it going anywhere."

He snapped to attention. "She's into Mr. Sands?"

"Yeah. But come on, he's a teacher! It's just a fantasy—she'll definitely get over it."

Ben flashed Jeremy a sympathetic grin. "Get used to it, man. They're *all* into him."

Jeremy's eyes wandered back to Amber, looking forlorn.

"Listen," I said, "we work at Triple Shot Betty's. You know where that is?"

He nodded, and some of the color returned to his face. "Yeah."

"You should come by. Maybe give her a CD or something. She likes . . . um . . . manga, and tattoos, of course, and . . ."

"Mr. Sands, apparently," he finished.

"Yeah, well, like I said, it's temporary. Believe me, if you can distract her, you'll be doing everyone a huge favor."

Jeremy turned to me, his expression grim. "Look, I appreciate what you're trying to do, but I think she's out of my league."

"Don't give up so easily!" Ben chided.

Jeremy managed a halfhearted grin.

"Seriously," I told him. "Come by Triple Shot Betty's. Amber whips up a killer mocha."

Jeremy shrugged. "Sure. Why not? What's a little more humiliation at this point?"

"That's the spirit!" I told him.

Sunday, January 18
9:20 P.M.

After we worked the morning shift at TSB, Amber and I came back to my house. I had to pound out a research paper for history—rough draft due tomorrow, so no more putting it off. Amber flipped through magazines and texted people while I worked. By four o'clock I'd read so many articles on the civil rights movement I thought my head would explode. I decided to take a quick MySpace break. Ha! Like most quick MySpace breaks, it turned into a four-hour detour.

My first mistake: I decided—just out of idle curiosity, mind you—to search for Mr. Sands. Suddenly, there he was, his default picture perfectly recognizable.

"Oh my God!" I yelped. "Mr. Sands is on MySpace!"

Amber pulled her chair so close she was practically in my lap. In a few seconds his profile loaded and there he was, staring up at us from the screen, his moody gray eyes boring into our souls.

"I love him," Amber whimpered. She leaned all the way forward and planted a kiss on the monitor.

"Down, girl," I said, but I have to admit his lips did look disturbingly kissable.

We pored over his profile, searching for pertinent details. He's 24, born October 30, a Scorpio (hot!). He went to high school in Carmel, did his undergraduate work at Stanford, his graduate work at UC Berkeley (impressive). His favorite movies are *Rear Window, Citizen Kane,* and *The Maltese Falcon* (classic). His musical taste ranges from Coltrane to Rogue Wave (eclectic).

Amber grabbed the mouse, logged herself in, and jerked the curser to his "add to friends" button.

"No, wait!" I protested.

"What?" Amber had that feverish look again. "Can't I friend him at least?"

"Let's think about this a second."

"What's there to think about?"

I leaned back in my chair. "Look, I'm not saying any of this is a good idea . . . but if you really want him, you've got to have a strategy."

She let go of the mouse. "What kind of strategy?"

"Here, let's look at your profile."

We went to Amber's page. Her pictures showed her in a variety of bad-girl poses. In her default pic she wore a skimpy little leopard-print bustier, her red hair streaming out wildly in all directions. Her smile looked crazed and demonic, while her fingers pointed at the camera in rocker-girl devil horns. It screamed *Underage freak looking for trouble.* Mr. Sands would take one look at it and hit "deny" to her friend request faster than you can say "jailbait."

"Don't take this the wrong way." I weighed my words carefully. "Your profile's cool and everything. I just don't think this is precisely the persona you should be projecting."

She leaned back and crossed her arms. "What do you mean?"

"You know how you asked me to, like . . . study him?"

She nodded.

"Well, I've been reading the books he's into and . . . you know, watching him carefully." I decided not to mention the rather involved fantasies I frequently indulge in while he's writing on the chalkboard—the ones where he and I end up in some smoky San Francisco jazz club.

"And . . . ?" she asked, impatient.

"He's like . . . an intellectual."

"So?"

"Well, right now your profile shrieks, 'I'm hot, reckless, and underage.'"

"Yeah?" Her tone said, *And your point is . . . ?*

"Look," I said, pointing at the monitor. "You've listed your interests as tattoos, fast cars, and death metal."

She shrugged. "Just being honest."

"Which is great. The thing is, with Mr. Sands, everything is based on a lie; you told him you're in college. If you want to get anywhere with him, you've got to build on that lie and add to it. I'm not endorsing it, I'm just saying if you want him, we've got to create an all-new you."

She squinted at me, mulling this over. "Okay, fair enough. So what should I change?"

I took another look at her tattoo slideshow and her Betty Page background. "Um, let's just start over, okay?"

An hour later, Amber had a brand-new profile. We kept her old one and just created a new, alternative Amber, one that's way more Mr. Sands–friendly. In this parallel universe she's a twenty-one-year-old lit major and philosophy minor at Brown taking a year off to care for her sick mother in Sonoma. Her interests include Jack Kerouac,

Zen Buddhism, Gary Snyder, and "the schism between self and society."

"What the hell does that mean?" she wanted to know.

I wasn't totally sure, but it was the sort of thing Mr. Sands was always going on about in class.

When we were almost done with her "About me" section, I had another thought. Maybe he'd get suspicious if we made her *too* much like him. She shouldn't be just a female version of Mr. Sands, after all—there had to be something else there, some opposites-attract ingredient. I decided to call on my own interests, since that's what I know most about. I added *Wuthering Heights* and *Jane Eyre* to her book list, and the sentence: "I'm partial to spooky, gothic literature and I gobble up the classics every chance I get."

Having completed the written portion of Project Pygmalion, we moved on to the eye candy. I didn't really know what a female beat was supposed to look like, so I just went for a generic intellectual motif and hoped it would do the trick. We raided Mom's closet and dressed Amber up in cashmere twinsets, tweed blazers, black turtlenecks, and plaid pleated skirts. We even put her in a black beret and showed her reading *On the Road*, her brow furrowed. She wore reading glasses and matte lipstick in serious shades like rose crepe and spiced raisin. By the time we'd loaded the photos onto her page, even I half believed in this fictional Amber who read *Dharma Bums* by candlelight and knew all about Zen Buddhism.

"Okay," I said, checking it over one last time for annoying grammatical errors. "Now you can friend him."

She brought up his page, chewing her bottom lip in

agitated concentration. She locked eyes with his photo as if engaging him in a staring contest. Then she swept the curser across the screen dramatically and clicked on his "Add to friends" button.

"Done," she said, turning to me, her cheeks pink and her eyes ablaze. "Now what?"

I leaned back in my chair and laced my fingers behind my head. "Now we wait."

Monday, January 19

1:30 A.M.

Grrrr. Woke up to the sound of Amber's ring tone. I'd only been asleep for forty minutes, since I'd had to stay up late writing that history paper after we got sidetracked by MySpace.

I answered the phone with, "Why?"

"He friended me! It worked! Oh my God, G, you're brilliant. I have to send him a message. What do I say?"

"Chill," I commanded.

"Please! You've got to help. I have to sound smart."

I rubbed my eyes. "Do not—I repeat—do not do anything."

"What? Why not?"

"Building the suspense. No message for a few days. Got it?"

"But—"

"No buts. Bye."

"G—"

"Hanging up now." And I did.

Good God, what have I gotten myself into?

Amber showed up at school today in a Wonder Woman
wig and massive sunglasses. I walked right past her the first
time, thinking absently, *Check out that girl's do.* It wasn't until
she called out, "Yo, G!" that I did a double take. There she
was, flashing her green eyes over the rim of her bug-eyed
shades.

"What are you doing?" I asked.

She pushed the sunglasses back into place and looked
around furtively. "You like?"

"Umm, Halloween's sort of over."

"I'm a brunette in the name of love."

"What does *that* mean?"

Her eyebrows shot up like this was the stupidest question
in the world. "Hello! There's someone on campus who can't
know I go here, or everything is totally ruined."

As if on cue, Mr. Sands came strolling down the hall,
delectable as ever, beat-up leather briefcase swinging from
one arm. When Amber saw him she whirled around, seized
a random locker, and started spinning the combination lock
madly.

"Coast is clear," I said when he'd passed. "Incidentally,
don't you think this is a little weird?"

"Did he look twice?"

"No, relax." I studied her carefully. "This is very strange,
Amber."

"What's strange?"

"Coming to school looking like . . ." I gestured helplessly

at her. "I mean, everyone thinks he's hot—doesn't mean you have to go all Lynda Carter on me."

She looked around quickly, then yanked her sunglasses off and fixed me with an anxious stare. "Geena, you don't understand. I've got it bad—I mean really, really bad. The whole John fiasco is nothing compared to this. Right now I'd rather throw myself in front of an eighteen-wheeler than ruin my chances with him."

"Okay, calm down—"

"He can't know I'm in high school. He just can't!" Her eyes were tinged with a distant, feverish look, like someone in a made-for-TV movie dying of some exotic, degenerative disease.

"Hey . . ." I squeezed her shoulder and tried to sound soothing. "Don't worry, okay? He'll never recognize you."

She brightened. "You think it's working?"

"If I didn't recognize you, there's no way he will."

"Good," she said, slipping her glasses back on. "Let's just try to keep it that way."

Tuesday, January 20
10:30 P.M.

> To: herolovespink@gmail.com
> From: skatergirl@yahoo.com
> Subject: Amber Alert
>
> Hey girl,
> Newsflash from Betty Land: Amber's totally lost it. She's crazy about this new English teacher named Mr. Sands.

Admittedly, the guy's cute. Okay, cute is an understatement, let's upgrade that to spine-tinglingly beautiful. But come on, he's a teacher! She's more likely to win a Pulitzer than get anywhere with him.

Okay, if I'm being totally honest, I have a slight case of Mr. Sands fever myself. He's just so intellectual and sophisticated and hip. I mean, Ben is smart—maybe even brilliant—but he doesn't have the worldly allure of Mr. Sands.

Does this ever happen to you? I mean, I know you're totally devoted to Claudio, but have you ever met a guy who speaks to a part of you Claudio can't reach? It's super confusing. Wish you were here. Miss you, Cuz . . .

Geena

To: skatergirl@yahoo.com
From: herolovespink@gmail.com
Subject: RE: Amber Alert

Geebs,
Oh, God, I'm tempted all the time! If you think it's rough staying committed to Ben, imagine what it's like having a boyfriend in Italy and living with A TON of gorgeous guys. Last year none of them even noticed me, but now that I have a boyfriend they find me fascinating. Just my luck. I know what you mean about the older man thing too. Remember when I had a crush on my piano teacher? Granted, I was nine, but still . . .

My advice: Don't freak. Just because you find Mr. Sands

*agréable doesn't mean you're unhappy with Ben. There's real
life, and then there's fantasy. Ben is real, Mr. Sands is a
fantasy. There's nothing wrong with having both.
Don't worry too much about Amber. Considering her train-
wreck-of-a-love-life, maybe indulging in a harmless, go-
nowhere crush isn't such a bad idea.*

Kisses,
Hero

Wednesday, January 21
11:40 P.M.

Amber's mom let her have the El Dorado tonight, so we figured we'd go hang at La Plaza Cafe for an hour or two. I
cruised into the living room to tell Mom where I was going. She and Mungo were sitting indecently close to each
other on the couch. They were gazing into each other's eyes
with such rapt attention, I felt sort of bad interrupting them.
I shouldn't have worried; neither of them even spared me a
glance.

"I'm going out with Amber," I announced.

"All right," Mom said.

"I'll be home by like ten thirty. Is that okay?"

"Mm-hm."

I decided to experiment. "Oh, and I'm thinking about join-
ing a cult. Saw it on the Internet—something about satanic
rituals, virgin sacrifices—pretty standard."

"Okay, babe. Sounds good," Mom answered.

Middle-Aged Love Zombies. What are you going to do?

As I climbed into the El Dorado, I told Amber, "I'd better not stay out too late."

"Why, what's up?"

"I have to get home before my mom does something regrettable with Mungo on the couch."

Amber nodded. "They're getting it on, huh?"

"Blegh. Let's not talk about it."

On our way to the cafe, we paused at an intersection and suddenly Amber let out an eardrum-rupturing squeal.

"Hello!" I complained. "I'd like to retain my hearing in that ear, thank you."

"That's him!" She pointed to the MG idling at the stop sign to our right.

As the MG rumbled into the intersection, I caught sight of Mr. Sands behind the wheel. My heart sped up in spite of my brain telling me it was no big deal.

Amber hit the gas and wrenched the steering wheel to the left, following his taillights.

"What are you doing? The cafe's that way." I pointed to our right, toward downtown.

"Cafe-Shmafe," she said, "we've got to see where he's going."

"Um . . . why?"

"Maybe he's going home!"

"And what? We're going to follow him in, make ourselves comfortable?"

She ignored me, concentrating instead on applying a coat of lip gloss while she drove. Never a good idea. A cat darted out into the road and she came inches from creaming it.

"Watch it!" I wailed.

Amber didn't even notice; between keeping tabs on Mr.
Sands and applying beauty products, she had no time for the
actual road. The MG turned left. She gave him a bit of a
lead before following, like a detective tailing a suspect. When
he pulled into the driveway of a two-storied, banana-yellow
bungalow, she slowed to a crawl, then parked on the opposite
side of the street. We watched in hushed silence as he let
himself in through the front door.

"Oh my God," Amber breathed. "This is where he lives."

The curtains were only partway drawn, and we could just
make out his blurred form passing through a slice of light.

"Uh, yeah, probably. Either that or he's breaking and en-
tering." Despite my patronizing tone, a quiet awe seeped into
my blood. I mean, we were at *Mr. Sands's* house. We were a
few measly yards from the inner sanctum of Dr. Hipster. I felt
a bit creepy violating his privacy, but that didn't stop me from
experiencing a little thrill.

"Come on," Amber said, opening her door.

"Wait—what are you—?" But she was already out of the
car. I scrambled out, taking care to close the heavy door
quietly.

"I just want to see where he lives." She started toward the
house.

"Are you crazy?" I whispered, scurrying after her.

"We won't get caught."

"Famous last words!" We were already to the front yard
now. Mr. Sands's head appeared in one of the windows, and
we both ducked.

Amber ran in a low crouch toward the side of the house,
and I had no choice but to follow. We hunched down below

a window, and suddenly a light came on inside. Amber poked her head up cautiously, but quickly squatted back down.

"He's in there," she whispered, her voice edged with barely contained hysteria. "I think it's his *bedroom*."

Inwardly, I groaned. This was against the law. I didn't think Yale admissions looked kindly on a police record. Just then, though, the light went out, and in a few moments a pair of French doors framed by a small balcony lit up above us.

"Pew. That smell!" I moved my foot and something clattered.

"Shhh!" Amber chided. "What was that?"

I gingerly reached down and retrieved the thing by my shoe. Holding it up, I read the label on the can as I mouth-breathed to avoid the rank odor: ALPO.

"Looks like Mr. Sands has got a—" But I didn't get to finish my sentence. I was interrupted by a low growl.

"Shit." Amber jumped behind me, gripping my arms and wielding me like a human shield. "That thing's huge."

"Niiice doggie. . . ." Before me, tense with warning, stood a waist-high, reddish-brown mutt. It growled again, its teeth glow-in-the-dark white. Over my shoulder I murmured to Amber, "They can smell fear, you know."

"Great. I bet I reek."

"We'd better go," I told her, "before it barks."

"I'm right behind you."

Naturally, the dog abandoned growls then for an explosive series of barks. The French doors upstairs swung open and we heard footsteps above us on the balcony.

I scurried over and hid behind a garbage can, but before Amber could wedge herself into the shadows beside me, an outside light came on and doused her face with incriminating brightness.

"Moriarty! Stop that. Oh, hi there."

She turned slowly and faced him, looking up. "Hi."

I bit my knuckles. *Busted!*

"Aren't you the girl from the coffee stand?" He sounded surprised, but not exactly hostile.

"Yeah. That's me."

My mind raced as I desperately tried to think up ways to make this seem, well, less stalker-ish, more . . . Romeo and Juliet. Or at least not restraining-order-worthy.

I leaned as close to her ear as I could without showing myself. "Tell him you live nearby."

"I live just a couple blocks from here," she told him.

"And you lost your cat . . ." I prompted.

"I lost my cat."

"Named Sal Paradise." Am I a genius, or what?

"His name's Sal Paradise. You haven't seen him, have you?"

I heard him chuckle, and I let out a sigh of relief. At least he wasn't calling the cops. "No, I don't think so."

"Oh. Okay."

"That's funny, though, isn't it?"

"What?" Amber sounded vaguely terrified.

"My dog and your cat are both characters from *On the Road.*"

Bull's-eye!

"Ohhhh," Amber trilled, laughing. "Yeah, that's funny. Okay, sorry to disturb you. See you later."

"Wait—did you find him?"

Amber was already moving toward the El Dorado, but paused to look back at him. "Who?"

"Sal Paradise."

"Uh—no, I think he's probably home already."

"Oh-kay." He sounded puzzled.

I just shook my head. Girl was blowing a beautiful opportunity. I watched hopelessly as she dashed for her car, opened the door, and dove in. I could see her banging her head against the steering wheel.

I waited until Mr. Sands had gone back inside and the dog had retreated to the other side of the yard before I slunk through the shadows and joined her.

⸰ • • ⸰ • ⸰

"Oh, my God!" Amber squealed as we sped back downtown in the El Dorado. "I thought I'd have a heart attack. He recognized me!"

"I know!" My heart was still racing.

"What was that about Paradise?"

"Main characters from *On the Road*?"

She gave me a blank look.

"Never mind."

She parked at a random spot on the plaza. The yuppie boutiques and restaurants were all closed, their windows staring out at the night with slick, hollow indifference. We sat in the shadowy depths of the El Dorado, trying to catch our breath.

Amber put her feet up on the dashboard and covered her eyes with her hands. "That was so embarrassing! How is this going to work? He's out of my league. You were right. The whole idea's insane."

A part of me felt relieved—finally, common sense was winning out. But then she spoke her next words, and I felt a little sick.

"He's got his doctorate and I'm just a trailer-trash nobody."

I squirmed. "Don't say that."

"Let's face it, Geena, it's people like me who'll be scrubbing toilets for people like him. We don't ride off into the sunset together."

This didn't sit right with me. If Amber had said anything else—he's too old for me, or I'm tired of wearing wigs, or just plain old never mind—I'd have been perfectly happy to drop it right there. But for her to give up on Mr. Sands because he was too smart, too Berkeley, too everything-she-wasn't, made me sad. To go along with that was to affirm all her worst assumptions about herself, and I just couldn't do it.

"I'm not saying I'm an expert in this area," I told her, "but if you want to get close to someone, you have to think like him, right?"

Even in the dark car, I could see that her sideways glance held equal parts hope and fear. "But that's just it. I have no idea how a guy like him thinks. He might as well be an alien."

"Well, we know he's in love with literature." I turned toward her in my seat. "Kerouac in particular—he's, like, obsessed with *On the Road*. What's that tell us?"

"*On the Road*? What's it about?"

"These guys who drive around a lot."

"What happens?"

"Basically, that's it. They drink and smoke and leave women all over the place."

"Sounds boring."

"A little." I rubbed my forehead, trying to concentrate. "Anyway, he's totally into the beats. They write sort of like jazz music, you know? Free and kind of crazy. So what's this predilection tell us about Mr. Sands?" I gazed through the windshield, turning the equation over in my mind. "Hip, irreverent, irresponsible? Infatuated with freedom?"

She nodded, her face pinched with worry. "O-kay . . ."

"See, if we know how he thinks—"

"Yeah, I get that, but come on. 'They drive around'? It's not much to go on."

"Well, the beats are like cultural icons, you know? They challenged the conventions of their day with radical ideas and created this revolutionary aesthetic—"

"I've got no idea what you're talking about." She hung her head, shrouding her face with a curtain of hair. "I'm not book smart like you."

"That's ridiculous!" I told her. "You're totally smart. You just have to let your inner nerdy girl out."

She laughed at that, and I felt better. I hate it when she gets on this *I'm stupid* kick. She's not exactly an intellectual, but she's still intelligent, and somehow it feels like my responsibility to prove that to her.

I glanced at my watch. "I should go—it's almost ten thirty. Who knows what's happening on our couch by now? Come over tomorrow after school, though. We'll work on that MySpace message."

"Okay." She sounded doubtful.

"We'll crack his code. Don't worry."

"You really think I can get him interested?"

How did this happen? Half the time I'm trying to pry her loose from this crazy Mr. Sands fixation, the other half I'm assisting in his seduction. Twisted.

"We'll give it a try," I promised.

Her face lit up with a smile. "Thanks, G." She turned the key in the ignition, and the El Dorado roared to life.

Thursday, January 22

2:15 P.M.

I saw Ben talking to Sophie during lunch. She had on this short, sexy little skirt, sheer tights, and shiny red patent-leather pumps that would have made me look like an underage crack whore, but somehow she pulled it all off with her usual panache. She was sitting with Marcy Adams in the cafeteria and Ben stood leaning against their table, chatting away. Every now and then Sophie would peek coquettishly up at him, bat her lashes (I'm so not kidding), then throw her head back and laugh as if whatever he'd just said was the hands-down most hilarious thing she'd ever heard in her life.

I told myself, *Just go over there. What's the big deal?* Somehow, though, I couldn't move my feet. All I could do was cower in the doorway, an icy cold dread creeping inch by inch up my spine like mercury rising slowly in a thermometer.

2:20 P.M.

In English class now, listening to Mr. Sands go on about Allen Ginsberg and his famous poem *Howl*. He read us part of it, but he says if he reads the whole thing he'll probably get fired. We're supposed to be finishing *Moby-Dick* this week, and then we're going to start *The Stranger*, but no matter what we're reading, Mr. Sands always finds a way to bring it back to his beloved beats.

Honestly, to me *Howl* just sounds like a bunch of words strung together. I keep slogging through *On the Road*, but I still don't really get what Mr. Sands is so excited about. I miss *Wuthering Heights*, *Jane Eyre*—give me a crazy chick in the attic and I'm good to go. These poems that careen wildly from one image to another and novels where the heroes just drive around kind of make me sleepy and carsick.

Well, if this *Howl* stuff is what he's into, I'm going to give it a try. For Amber's sake. If I'm really going to help her with that MySpace message, I should make it good, right? I mean, how hard can it be? Just start stringing words together, right?

I saw the best minds of my English class destroyed by their hysterical desire to sound like some drugged-out dude with a beard

Okay, that's not good. We're not going for parody here. Start over.

I saw you outside the Floating World
In your T-shirt faded to threadbare sunshine
Your hair a nimbus of light
And in your eyes of molten moss
A thousand fractured reflections of my dreams drifted slowly.

Too much of a love poem already—good-bye *Howl*, hello Harlequin. As far as I can tell, there's nothing very romantic about the beats. That's why it's so hard to use them as a blueprint for how to seduce your English teacher.

Oh, God. Mr. Sands just called on me, and I had no idea

what he was asking. How horrifying! I better put this away before he confiscates it, forcing me to commit *seppuku* right here with my number two pencil.

7:45 P.M.

Rain lashed against the windows as Amber sat on my bed, impatiently drumming her fingers on my laptop.

"G! We've been sitting here for over an hour. How hard can it be to write one little MySpace message?"

I looked up from where I sat hunched over a notebook on my floor, surrounded by beat poem printouts, Kerouac books, and crumpled wads of paper. I'd already been through ten stabs at poems, each more miserable and ridiculous than the last. I was starting to think that a totally lame "Thanks for the add!" comment on his page would have to do, when suddenly Amber clutched the screen.

"Oh my God! It's him! He just sent me a message!"

"Seriously?" I jumped up from the floor and dove beside her on the bed, devouring the words on the screen.

Hi, Amber. Are you by any chance the girl from the coffee shack—the one with a cat named Sal Paradise?

"He's online right now! What do I say?" She bugged her eyes at me and a vein at her temple throbbed like it might burst.

"Here." I reached over and scooped the Mac off her lap, pulling it onto mine, then hit reply.

That's me. Sorry about Sal; he's a little too much like his namesake— always restless. Is your dog anything like Dean Moriarty? If so, I bet he's got illegitimate puppies stashed all over the neighborhood.

Before I could second-guess myself, I hit SEND.

"Wait, who's Dean Moriarty again?" Amber asked.

"Just a little Kerou-wackiness." I felt giddy, thinking of him reading my words.

In just a few minutes, a new message came through, and I clicked on it hungrily. Amber squeezed my arm so tightly she cut off the circulation.

LOL. Fortunately, my Moriarty is fixed, so he doesn't have that problem. I should have named him Ginsberg, since he definitely knows how to Howl—ha, ha! I see from your profile you're taking a year off from Brown. How's that going?

Amber closed her eyes in ecstasy. "Oh, my God. It's happening. It's happening!"

I typed as quickly as I could.

It's okay. Slow-noma is a little dull, though. I miss talking about books and plays and good films with people who actually THINK.

After I hit SEND, there was a longish pause. I worried I'd gone too far—did that seem too elitist? Worse yet, did he think I was fishing for an invitation?

Amber chewed on a fingernail. "What's taking so long?"

Just then, another message came through, and we both leaned closer to the screen, hardly breathing.

I know exactly what you mean. I left Berkeley so I could work on my dissertation in peace, but I'm going a little nuts. It's all wine-obsessed yuppies and their yabies up here.

My fingers flew across the keyboard.

What are yabies?

His reply came quickly.

Yabies=Yuppie babies. I just made that up!

LOL, I wrote.

I'm subbing at the high school, so I teach the yabies, and let me tell you, they're about as intellectual as a bag of hammers.

Ouch! I wanted to ask him about Geena Sloane's recent essay on Melville—didn't it show startling academic promise? Wasn't her thesis daring, her conclusion incendiary?

Amber clutched my arm again. "Can you get him to ask me out?"

I thought for a few seconds before typing my response.

You poor thing! I went to SVHS, so I know what you're talking about. I'm so starved for good conversation, I've taken to chatting on MySpace . . .

I hit SEND. We sat there, staring at the screen, for what seemed like an eternity. Finally, his message came through.

Maybe we should get together for coffee sometime.

Amber screamed so loudly, my mom's footsteps came pounding and she pushed open the door without knocking.

"What's wrong?" she panted. "What happened?"

Oh, nothing, Mom, we're just seducing our English teacher. Go back to making out with your Scottish soccer champ. "Nothing. Just working on an essay."

She raised an eyebrow at that, but since there was no blood or hypodermic needles visible, she shut the door and presumably returned to Mungo-land.

Yeah, I typed. *That would be cool.*

Are you free Sunday afternoon? he replied.

Amber flopped facedown on the bed this time and screamed into a pillow.

"Should I take that as a yes?" I asked her.

She squirmed back up into a sitting position. "I get off at four."

Is four fifteen okay? I typed.

Perfect. Four fifteen at La Plaza, then?

Sounds good.

After we logged off, I put the laptop on the floor and joined Amber in a hyphy little jump-a-thon. We bounced up and down on my bed until our heads grazed the ceiling and our giggles got so manic that my mom appeared in my doorway again.

"Still working on that essay?" she asked dryly.

"Yep," I said.

"I'm in love!" Amber blurted out.

Mungo appeared behind Mom then, wrapping his arms around her waist; they stood there watching us with wry little smiles and I knew that if she weren't so smitten, she'd be scolding us about destroying the bedsprings.

"Looks like you've got your hands full," Mungo said in his funny accent. "Couple a girls in love? That spells trouble."

I knew he was right, especially since it's not entirely clear who's in love with whom.

Friday, January 23
6:20 P.M.

Dad called tonight and we talked for about twenty minutes. I think he might be a little wigged about Mom and Mungo. When he asked where she was and I said out, he asked who with and I told him. He got all quiet then.

"Are they spending a lot of time together?" he asked finally.

"Does 'attached at the hip' mean anything to you?"

He made this kind of funny sound, something between a cough and a sigh. "You think they're . . . serious?"

"I guess." On the surface, I felt pretty calm, but somewhere in the back of my brain, sirens were going off. If there's one thing offspring should never have to do, it's inform one parental unit about the sex life of the other.

Luckily, he changed the subject before we moseyed too far down that road. "Listen, I'm going to be up there in a couple weeks for work. Will you be around?"

We filled the rest of the conversation with logistics—figuring out when we'd get together, what we'd do, that sort of stuff. With Dad, there has to be some sort of activity planned, a minor event; otherwise the awkward pauses get too, well, awkward. He didn't mention bringing Jen with him, for which I am eternally grateful. A few Jen-free hours with Dad might be just what I need.

Sunday, January 25
1:20 A.M.

Mom was out on a date with Mungo tonight, so Ben brought over a movie—*Something of the Something-Something Zombies*—and we kicked it on the couch with a bowl of popcorn.

How are you supposed to know what kind of kisser you are? I mean, I know he's good, but I've got no idea how I rate. If it's good for me, does that mean it's good for him? I could write a five-page paper on the softness of his lips, the cinnamon scent of his breath, the crazy heat that swirls through me like static electricity inside a dryer when he nibbles on my bottom lip—that stuff I'm sure about. But I've got absolutely no clue how it feels on his end. It's like listening to your own voice while you're talk-ing, or imagining your face without a mirror—impossible.

I guess since he keeps on kissing me I'm not a total failure at it; he's never pulled away in horror or gagged or anything. But then, aren't guys so perpetually sex-starved that making out with a slab of tuna would still be better than getting no action at all?

We'd been going at it since the opening credits, and I was vaguely aware of a zombie apocalypse shaping up on screen, when slowly—so slowly that I barely noticed it at first—Ben's hand floated up from his lap and touched my breast with such tentative hesitation that he might have been testing the volt-age of an electric fence. I couldn't help it; I laughed right into his mouth.

"What?" he pulled back and looked at me, his eyebrows all akimbo.

"Nothing, I just—nothing."

"Now you've got to tell me, or I'll be paranoid."

"It's just—you can—" I tripped over my half-formed thoughts. My lips tingled from all the kissing.

Now he laughed. "Thanks. That explains everything."

"No, I just meant, you don't have to be so . . ." I glanced down at my chest, then back up at his face. ". . . tentative."

He squinted at me like I was an equation he was trying to solve. "Last time I was here—in the kitchen? I got the feeling you were kind of weirded out."

"Really?" Of course he was right, but I wasn't sure I wanted to admit it.

"I don't want to rush things." He ran his knuckles lightly along my cheekbone. "What's the hurry?"

Suddenly it felt like the perfect time to ask him something I'd been wondering about for a while. "Ben, can I ask you a question?"

He nodded. "Okay."

"Have you—are you . . . what I mean is . . ."

He chuckled. "Am I a virgin?"

"Yeah."

"Pretty much."

Now it was my turn to laugh. "I don't think it's a 'pretty much' kind of thing. It's more a yes or a no."

"Okay, then yes, I'm a virgin. I mean I've done . . . stuff . . . but never that."

I could feel my face going tight. As far as I knew, Ben had never had a girlfriend before—at least, nobody at SVHS. "Who did you do 'stuff' with?"

He leaned back against the couch and sighed. Uh-oh. I could feel something inside me—maybe my heart—plummeting like a kamikaze. I just knew I wasn't going to like what was coming. I wanted to yank the question back and shove it down my throat so he'd never have to answer.

"Don't trip on this, okay?" His dark eyes pleaded with me. "It's really not a big deal."

I just nodded, not trusting my voice.

"You know how Sophie's parents are friends with my parents?"

I nodded again, unable to look at him now.

"Well, about a year ago our families spent Christmas break together? Up in Tahoe?"

He was turning every statement into a question. Why was

he doing that? I dug my fingernails into my arm, urging myself not to cry.

"Sophie's family has a place up there? Anyway, we messed around, but it was totally a one-time thing, I swear. I'm not interested in her at all."

Annoyingly, I felt that stinging tingle in my nose that always happens right before I cry. "So that's why she's always flirting with you."

"No—really, we're just friends. She's like that with everyone."

"Uh-huh." I stood up.

"Geena, please."

"I'm fine." I stepped away from him. "I just have to pee."

I locked myself in the bathroom and stared into the mirror. Who was I kidding? I could never compete with Sophie De Luca. She'd already done "stuff" with Ben—more than *we'd* done, obviously. A barrage of images sloshed through my brain, all of them queasy-making.

Why was Ben even with me? I thought about that for a moment. He didn't know she would move back here. By the time she did, we'd already gotten together, and he's too nice of a guy to dump me just because he wants some other girl. She's caviar and I'm Cheez Whiz, but he doesn't have the heart to tell me that.

"Geena?" Ben knocked softly at the door. "You okay?"

He totally pities me. Must not be pitiful. A tear leaked out and I swiped at it, irritated at my lack of self-control. "Yeah. Be out in a second."

I heard his footsteps heading back toward the living room.

After a few minutes I pulled myself together and went

out there again. As soon as I sat beside him on the couch, I jabbed at the remote control before he could ask me anything. I knew if we started talking about it again I'd break down, and that was something I simply couldn't afford.

8:40 P.M.

Amber and I worked the zombie shift this morning—get there at six, open at six thirty. Brutal. Ben went home last night around one, and the measly four hours of sleep I'd managed to catch just weren't enough. The morning took on a surreal, underwater quality. Even my double mocha wasn't enough to cut through the blurry delirium. Amber, on the other hand, was wide-awake. Usually she's wicked cranky when we get there, but this morning she was so psyched about her pending coffee date with Mr. Sands, she couldn't stop talking.

"Isn't he cute? God, he's so adorable!" She opened her wallet again and toyed with the plastic photo holder. She'd actually printed out a little picture of him from MySpace and tucked it in there, which I find kind of mortifying. Amber's really cool under normal circumstances, but when it comes to Mr. Sands she's just this side of psycho.

"Yeah," I said flatly. "He's cute."

She chewed on the straw in her iced latte. "I'm freaking out. I mean, what if he asks me something about—what's it called again?"

"*On the Road?*"

"Yeah, that. What do I say?"

"I doubt he'll quiz you." I didn't want to say it out loud, but frankly I was pretty worried too. Just about anything Mr.

Sands might want to talk about posed a threat to Amber's credibility. She's supposed to be taking a year off from Brown. It's pretty hard for a girl who's never read anything more intellectual than the juicy parts in *Valley of the Dolls* to fob herself off as an Ivy League Lit Major.

"Maybe you should just steer the conversation away from books," I said. "Tell him about your sick mom or something."

"My sick—?" She looked puzzled, then remembered. "Oh, right, my sick *mom*. That's a real turn-on."

"At least you won't sound stupid."

A look of hurt flashed across her face, and I instantly regretted my choice of words.

"I didn't mean it like that."

She chewed the straw again. "No, you're right. I'm going to look like an idiot. This is crazy! What were we thinking? I can't go!"

"Amber!" I put my hands on her shoulders. "Look at me. You're bright and funny and beautiful. What more could he ask for?"

She took a deep breath and exhaled slowly. "Okay. I can do this."

"Of course you can."

We heard a car driving into the parking lot. The motor coughed and then, as if conjured by our thoughts, Mr. Sands's head appeared, framed perfectly in the window. He had on mirrored sunglasses and as he turned to us, smiling, I felt my heart go all hummingbird-fluttery. I expected Amber to cata-pult toward him, bubbling over with cleavage and giggles; instead she just stared, eyes wide, unmoving.

Seeing she wasn't budging, I hurried over and slid open

the window. He looked so good there in the morning sunlight, bundled up against the cool air in a navy blue pea coat. He propped his sunglasses up on his head and his gray eyes seemed extra-piercing.

"Can I . . . um . . . help you?" I managed.

"Morning, Geena."

"Hi." Hearing him say my name made my stomach turn over.

"Happy Sunday."

"Yeah," was my incredibly urbane and witty response.

"Hi, Amber." He waved at her. "How you doing?"

"Okay," she croaked.

After an awkward pause he asked, "Are one of you lovely baristas thinking about taking my order?"

"Oh. Right." I flashed a look at Amber to see if she wanted to, but she seemed paralyzed, so I took charge. "What would you like?"

"Double latte, lots of foam."

"To go?" As soon as I said it, I desperately wanted to take it back.

He looked around. "Is there some other option?"

"No." My blush-o-meter skyrocketed.

"To go, then."

"No problem." I set to work on his drink, shooting Amber *Get over there* looks the whole time.

She finally managed to trudge across our microscopic workspace to the window. "Hi."

Her approach was so soundless and her greeting so loud that Mr. Sands, absorbed in his rearview mirror, actually flinched when she spoke. "Oh, hi!"

"Hi," she repeated, as tonelessly as before.

"So, you still want to hang out this afternoon?"

A moment passed as I put a lid on his latte and held my breath, afraid to turn around.

"Yeah. Definitely. You?"

"Of course." He lowered his voice to a confiding tone. "I'm kind of starved for conversation these days, myself. I'm looking forward to it."

I waited for Amber—usually so adroit at flirtation—to fill the awkward silence with a pithy comeback. I thought maybe she was timing it carefully, like Mae West waiting a beat before she delivers her throaty invitation. Nope. Amber just stood there, blushing! I've never seen Amber blush. It was unnatural. Finally she said, "Yeah, well, me too."

"Here's your latte," I said, sweeping in with his drink.

"Oh, great. Thanks." He fished in his pockets for money, came out with a crumpled fiver. I took it from him and rang him up while Amber shuffled away into the shadows.

"That's three twenty-five," I said. "Here's your change."

"Keep it," he murmured absently.

"Thanks, Mr. Sands!" I was all gee-whiz innocence. This guy has a talent for bringing out the socially retarded in all of us, apparently.

"You're welcome. See you later on, Amber." Then he put the MG into gear and cruised slowly away, searching his rearview mirror the whole time.

I turned to Amber. "What was that?"

Her cat eyes flashed.

"Don't look at me like that! I've just never seen you so tongue-tied."

She let out her breath like she'd been underwater for way too long. "I suck."

"No, no, no. Let's not be negative. Maybe less is more. He's probably deeply intrigued by your mysterious, taciturn ways."

"Taciturn?"

"SAT word. Sorry."

"Shit. Now that he thinks I'm smart, I'm terrified to open my mouth."

"You'll get over that. You just got shy. I know it never happens to you, but most of us get like that at least once a week." I turned to the espresso machine and started whipping up a couple comfort beverages: mocha for me, latte for her. "Oh my God, I never thought of this before, but you're the same drink."

"What?" She looked at me like I was insane.

"You're both into lattes! That would be a really interesting way to gauge compatibility. You know, like astrology, Betty style. Ben likes milk shakes, though. What's that mean?" I tried to remember what Sophie had ordered when she stopped by in her shiny birthday Mercedes. Then I pictured her in a fetching little parka, prancing through the snow, and I felt sick.

"I can't do this!" Amber started banging her head gently against the wall. "Why am I cursed? I'm in love with someone I can't talk to."

"Don't do that. Brain damage isn't going to help your cause."

"Geena!" She seized my arm so suddenly I almost spilled the shot I was pouring. "You have to help me! I can't do this alone."

"What do you want me to do? Hide under the table and feed you lines?"

She considered this a moment. "You think that'd work?"

"No. Okay? No, I don't. Are you insane?"

"G, please." Her green eyes were moist now. "Just this one time?"

I sighed, stirring an extra squirt of chocolate into my mocha. "You promise, if I help you out this once—and I'm not saying it'll work—you won't expect it next time? Because this could get old pretty quick."

"All I need is a little backup—until we get to know each other. Then I can relax and be myself. I mean, I'm not stupid, right?" Her expression begged for reassurance. "Once he gets to know me, he'll see that. Won't he?"

"Of course." I handed over her latte. I didn't want to get more involved in this whole fiasco, but I didn't want to let her down either. *Maybe she's right,* I told myself. *If I just get her through this first date, she'll shed her insecurities and be fine. She might not even be so crazy about him after this—they have nothing in common, after all—and then we can just drop the whole thing.*

"Please?" she whispered.

"All right," I told her, "listen up. Here's what we're going to do . . ."

° ● ● ° ● °

Eight hours later, I found myself sitting at La Plaza Cafe in dark glasses and Amber's itchy, humiliating wig. My cell phone sat in my lap, ready for action.

About four feet away, at the next table, Amber and Mr. Sands were just sitting down, steaming lattes in hand. Luckily Mr. Sands took a seat with his back to me, and Amber positioned herself so I could see her face. She looked like she wanted to heave. Well, it was a first date; anyone would be a little on edge.

I thought of all the bad press MySpace gets—a pedophile's buffet and all that. Ha! Sometimes underage girls are the predators, not the prey.

"So, Amber, you're from Sonoma, right?"

Good, starting with very easy questions. I could hear Mr. Sands clearly, even though the place was pretty crowded. Luckily, there was no one I really knew in there; I recognized a couple freshmen girls sucking down milk shakes toward the back, but I couldn't tell you their names, and they didn't even look at me. Mostly it was populated by weekend tourists— middle-aged, paunchy wine people with expensive clothes and sour faces.

"Yeah," Amber said.

"So, what do you think of Sonoma?"

"I like it. It's kind of boring, but it's okay."

He nodded. "I know. I'm climbing the walls. How did you like Providence?"

I held my breath. Would she guess that's where Brown is? "It's . . . nice."

That's right, I urged inside my head. *Vague is good. Keep it vague.* Meanwhile I sent a text as fast as I possibly could: *Prvdnc=cld, est cst, brwn.*

She glanced at her lap, then looked up quickly. "It's Brown. I mean, it's cold."

I cringed. This wasn't going well. If I couldn't feed her lines about the weather, how would I fare when we hit Kerouac's original scroll versus the edited manuscript? What if he started talking existentialism or Dadaists or—oh, God. This plan had holes you could drive a truck through.

Just then my phone chirped and Mr. Sands turned his head slightly, but didn't actually look at me. I studied the screen; it was a text from Ben. *Miss you. What's up?*

Argh! Quickly I replied: *Busy now, talk later.*

I heard Mr. Sands chuckle. "Yeah, well, the East Coast tends to be that way—cold, I mean. What about Brown? You were a lit major, right? Did you like your classes? Are you going back?"

She nodded and chewed her bottom lip. Surely she could improvise with this one. "Oh, yeah. I liked it. There were so many great teachers and . . ." Her face clouded over momentarily, as if she'd lost her train of thought, but then she blurted out, "Smart people."

Okay, okay. Not great, but not tragic. My fingers hovered at the ready, waiting for a more specific question. It was like some sort of twisted tag-team game show. I started to sweat under the hideous wig.

"I went to Berkeley for grad school, but I thought about Brown," he said. "I hear they have a good lit program. What's your area of interest?"

"Area of interest?" she echoed.

"Yeah—I mean, what sort of stuff do you like to read?"

I decided to bank on my "opposites attract" theory. *Bronte,* I texted her.

"Bront," she said.

"Bront?" he repeated.

Bront-ay, I wrote.

"I mean, Brontaaay." She drew out the second syllable so

it sounded, if possible, even more ridiculous than *Bront*.

I wanted to slink under the table, but I was too busy texting. *U lk Emily bst.*

"Which one?" he asked, and I wanted to punch the air. Finally, I'd predicted one of his questions and gotten there first.

"Emily."

"Aha. So you like that gothic stuff, huh? Ghosts and moors and all that?"

She laughed coquettishly. "I guess."

Okay, this was better. They were teasing each other, at least. A tiny ray of hope. *Ask abt JK*, I wrote. It was risky, but I figured she couldn't keep glancing down at her lap every five seconds or he'd get suspicious. We had to get him talking, and I knew nothing would get him on a roll like good ol' Jack.

"Are you just kidding?" she asked.

Jack Kerouac! I wrote, my fingers jabbing at the phone violently.

She glanced down again, her expression slightly panicked. Then she slapped on a smile and said, "I mean, you weren't kidding when you said you really like Jack Kerouac, were you? You . . . love his books, don't you?"

Mr. Sands leaned back in his chair and looked up at the ceiling. "Oh, God, don't get me started."

Please, I begged, *get started. Get started and keep going; my thumbs are cramping.*

And then, as if the gods of carpal tunnel heard my prayer, he started talking Kerouac. He got all wrapped up in it, just like he does in class. Amber only had to nod, and smile, and giggle on occasion. He required nothing more. Slowly, she relaxed, and even seemed to be having fun. She was his willing audience, his fascinated pupil, and under her adoring gaze he became more eloquent, more passionate than ever.

He'd been going for like twenty minutes without a pause. I figured I'd done my duty and could now skedaddle. Sure, it was fun sitting that close to Mr. Sands, staring at the back of his head, his perfect neck, the outline of his shoulder blades beneath his threadbare T-shirt, but after a while I got bored. I'd already heard all of this stuff in class more than once—about how Kerouac supposedly holed up in some Manhattan apartment for three weeks and wrote *On the Road* as a long, single-spaced paragraph on eight sheets of tracing paper, blah, blah, blah. I signaled to Amber that I was leaving, tucked my cell phone into my pocket, and headed for the door.

"But you already know all this, right? I mean, you named your cat after the main character. What do *you* like about his work?"

I stopped dead in my tracks.

"Oh, I think he's . . . a-amazing," Amber stammered. Even from across the room, I could sense her confidence evaporating. "He's so . . . smart."

"Exactly," Mr. Sands enthused. "God, it's great to meet a girl who gets this. Most of the women in my graduate program *hated* Kerouac. They thought he was an overrated, self-absorbed misogynist."

Whew, I thought. *Close call.*

"Why do you think so many women just don't get him?"

Damn, another question. Could she sidestep it?

"I don't know." Amber paused. I turned around and saw her face going white. "Maybe because women aren't really as into . . . cars? I mean, I like cars. A lot. I like . . . driving around."

That was it. We were doomed.

On impulse I ripped off my wig, stuffed it the best I could into the pocket of my hoodie, and strolled over to their table. "Hi, Amber! Oh, wow, Mr. Sands. How's it going? Fueling up on more caffeine, huh? Feeling twitchy yet?"

Mr. Sands looked momentarily put out, like he didn't particularly want to run into one of his "yabie" students right then. *Oh, yeah?* I wanted to say. *Well, for your information, you're having coffee with my brainchild. I invented this Brontë-loving redhead.*

"How's it going, Geena?" He offered a small, tight smile, then his eyes moved to my sweatshirt and he looked disgusted. "What's that?"

I glanced down and saw several tufts of wig hair spilling out of my pocket. I tried to stuff them out of sight. "Pet hamster. So annoying." *Random!* "Hey, I'm sorry to interrupt, but Amber, did you drive here?"

She nodded. "Uh-huh."

"Could I get a ride? My friend ditched me and I've got to get home prontissimo or my mom's going to kill me." It was the best I could offer on the spur of the moment.

"Oh. Um . . ." She glanced at Mr. Sands, who didn't look happy. "I guess I could."

Yeah, you'd better, unless you want to wax poetic about how you've unraveled the mysteries of Kerouac because you "like cars."

When we got out to the street, she looked at me. "That didn't go too well, huh?"

I shook my head. "You think he could tell you were texting?"

"Don't know. I don't think so."

"Let's not try this stunt again, okay? Totally stressful. Plus that wig itches!"

She giggled. "'Pet hamster'! What was that?"

I couldn't help laughing too. "I panicked!"

I'm a little worried about where all this is headed. Amber shows no signs of backing off, despite the obvious fact that they would make a *hopeless* couple. Somehow, she doesn't seem to get that. It's like, who cares that they can't have a conversation? She's still "in love" with him, whatever that means.

What would it be like if Mr. Sands and I could just talk? What if we could order coffee, sit down, and have a real conversation—not as student and teacher, but as equals? I'd love to tell him why women don't get Kerouac. (Hello? Maybe because Kerouac's female characters are about as three-dimensional as paper dolls?) Mr. Sands's and Amber's differences go way beyond the usual Mars versus Venus; they're not even orbiting the same sun. The only real compatibility here is between my mind and his.

Not that I care about that, really. I mean, I have a boyfriend. Of course, he's secretly in love with a beautiful beeatch who's determined to come between us. Also, he seems more interested in my boobs lately than my mind. Still, he's my boyfriend, and Mr. Sands is my English teacher.

Must remember that.

Monday, January 26
9:20 P.M.

Amber came over today after school. The first thing she did was check her MySpace page, naturally. Mr. Sands had already messaged her again. We read it together as she squeezed my fingers, breathing so hard I feared she'd hyperventilate.

Hey Amber! Had fun yesterday spending time with you. Too bad we got interrupted, I really enjoyed our conversation. Want to meet up again some day this week?

Amber went into such a state after reading this, I thought I'd have to restrain her. She started swiveling her hips like a demented go-go dancer, singing this Propeller Head song we always listen to at work. "He's got a nice body. He's wearing velvet pants. He's got a nice body. He's wearing velvet pants."

"He's got a comma splice in there," I grumbled.

She stopped and looked at me. "What?"

"The guy's an English teacher! He should know better."

"What crawled up your butt and died?"

"I'm just saying—grammar matters."

She raised an eyebrow and stared me down until I had no choice but to look at her. "You're mad," she said. "Why?"

"I'm not mad." Okay, she was sort of right; I wasn't happy. But the compost pile of feelings inside me couldn't be described as simply "mad."

A part of me felt smug. My plan had worked. We'd fobbed her off as an Ivy League sophisticate, and that was all my doing. And mixed in with my smugness lurked this tiny sprout that was more *swoon* than *I-told-you-so*. After all, Mr. Sands isn't just asking Amber out on a second date. He's interested in Amber's body and *my* mind, which is flattering—at least, uh, half flattering.

But the thing that makes me grumpy is I do all the work and she gets all the credit. Mr. Sands sees me as this annoying "interruption," while she gets to be Sex Goddess avec Mega-Brain.

"Okay, fine. Don't tell me. What do we write back?" Amber hopped onto my bed and continued her manic go-go routine up there, singing that ridiculously repetitive song again. "He's got a nice body. He's wearing velvet pants."

My cell rang. I looked at the caller ID and saw that it was Ben. I just couldn't deal right then, so I turned it off. The situation with Mr. Sands required my full attention. I had to disentangle myself before it got even more complicated.

I looked at Amber. "Maybe you should take it from here."

She froze. "What do you mean?"

"I just feel sort of weird, writing him for you."

"You don't have to write him for me." She sounded insulted. "Just help me out, like you did before."

Ha! *Just help me out?!* Who was she kidding?

"Okay, let's do it this way: You write it, then I'll take a look. Like an editor."

Her expression told me this wasn't what she had in mind, but by then her pride had kicked in. "Fine."

She settled down at the computer, and after a while her fingers started tapping at the keyboard. I dug out some history homework and tried to lose myself in a chapter on JFK, but I found Amber a little distracting. She kept trying different positions as she sat at my desk chair—straddling it backward, perching on it in a sort of squat, hugging her knees. Every two minutes or so she'd let out a gusty sigh. Finally I closed my book and peered over her shoulder.

"How's it going?"

She shook her head. "I suck at this, G."

I looked at the screen.

Hi Rex! How are you! I am fine! I would luv another meating with you!!!

"Okay," I said, trying to be diplomatic. "That's a good start."

She looked up at me, cringing. "Can you fix it?"

I really couldn't resist. Amber needed me. Also, I detest bad punctuation. Excessive exclamation marks are particularly revolting, like a squad of crazed cheerleaders infusing every sentiment with mad perkiness.

I scooted her out of the way and sat down at the computer. She hovered, which made me nervous.

"Will you go see if we have anything good to eat?" I gestured toward the kitchen. "I'm starving."

"Sure, but don't send it until I see it, okay?"

"Roger that."

By the time she got back with a bag of Doritos and two sodas, I'd composed the following:

Dear Rex,
I had a great time too. My favorite things in life are strong
coffee and scintillating conversation. I've been thinking
more about Kerouac and why, as you said, lots of women

readers don't "get" him. I suspect it has to do with his female characters. They tend to lurk in the background, thinly developed and blurry. What I like about JK is the freedom of his prose; he writes with a breathless sense of wonder, you know? Anyway, we got interrupted, so I didn't have time to explain my take. I'd love to get together again this week. Let me know what works for you.

> *Amber*

"What's 'scintillating'?" Amber asked through a mouth full of chips.

"Interesting. Fascinating."

She shrugged. "If you say so. It's not too . . . ?"

"Too what?"

"Too . . . you know . . . pretentious?"

I read it again. "You want me to change *scintillating* to *fascinating*?"

"No, actually, I think it's good. Let's just send it." Impulsively, she reached over and jabbed the cursor at the SEND button.

We looked at each other, wide-eyed, both of our faces telegraphing exactly the same thought: *Oh, God, what have we done?*

Tuesday, January 27
5:20 P.M.

Amber and I loitered by her locker after school today. A couple sophomore girls were hanging a big banner with bloodred, bubbly letters announcing the Valentine's dance. Great! Another sadistic high school ritual to survive. Amber modeled her new wig for me, a Farrah Fawcett confection she picked up at the Goodwill. I don't really get how she can stand to wear a rug that's crawling with lice for all we know, but I didn't bring it up. She's already informed me that most wigs cost more than she makes at TSB all month, so snagging one for a buck-fifty's a coup.

We cracked ourselves up turning the wig around so she looked like Chewbacca on bleach. When I heard a familiar voice behind me, though, my laughter died in my throat.

"Geena—hey. You got a minute?"

I turned around so fast, whiplash threatened to immobilize me. "Mr. Sands. Hi."

Amber yanked the wig back around and practically dove inside her locker, choking on a fit of giggles.

Mr. Sands shot a quizzical glance at her back and said, "Sorry—didn't mean to interrupt."

"No, not at all," I said. "*Dorothy* and I were just hanging out. What's up?"

He cut his eyes to "Dorothy," who dug furtively in her locker like a determined mole, then very subtly tilted his head away from her in a "Let's go over there so we won't be overheard by this wack-job" look. *Oh God*, I thought wildly, *he knows. He knows I cooked up her profile, that Amber's in high school and we're both irrationally obsessed with him. Good-bye Yale, good-bye dignity, hello suspension, restraining order, and stalking charges!*

We walked out of earshot and he studied me carefully. "First, I want to tell you your essay on *Moby-Dick* blew everyone else's out of the water."

"Really? Wow." I could feel my face getting hot. "Really?"

He grinned. "Of course. You surprised?"

"Well, yeah—I mean—sort of—"

"I'm surprised you're surprised. You seem so self-assured on paper. Your work has full-ride-scholarship written all over it."

A molten lump of pure joy lodged itself in my chest. I stood there paralyzed, unable to speak. I saw myself at Yale with Mr. Sands beside me, toting books, smiling encouragement. We would be young lovers in our Ivy League Camelot, living on literature, drunk on words.

Just then I spotted Ben walking toward us. He shot me a curious look, but when he saw my expression his face clouded over with worry and he pivoted slightly to detour around us. God only knows what my traitorous eyes telegraphed this time. I was such a miserable girlfriend! Then I pictured Ben and Sophie throwing snowballs at each other, and I felt a little less guilty. Sure, I *thought* about Mr. Sands, but he'd actually messed around with Sophie.

I tuned back in to Mr. Sands just in time to catch his question. "Incidentally, ah, your friend Amber . . . at the coffee place? You know her very well?"

The smoldering hunk of happiness inside me was snuffed out completely. "Pretty well."

"You two probably have a lot to talk about." He tried hard to sound light and breezy.

"How do you mean?"

"Since you're both such avid readers."

"Oh," I mumbled. "Yeah."

It didn't seem like such a big deal, lying to him on MySpace, but somehow standing here face-to-face I felt a thousand times more culpable.

"She's taking a year off from Brown, right?"

For a crazy, sweaty moment I felt tempted to tell him the truth. Then I saw Amber shoot me a stealthy look from under her mop of ratty blond synthetic locks and I knew I couldn't do that to her.

"Yeah. Her mom's sick."

"Right. That's what she said." He didn't sound too concerned. And okay, so we made it all up, but it seemed like he should at least fake an interest in Amber's life, right? Then he ran a hand through his hair and looked at me in a way that made it impossible to see him as anything but perfect. "Do you happen to know . . . um . . . how old she is?"

Translation: Is she jailbait?

"Like twenty-one, I think. She'll be a senior when she goes back."

He nodded in a just wondering, casual way, but he looked so relieved I thought he might break into an involuntary jig. "Great. Well, anyway, keep up the good work. I'll see you tomorrow."

○ ● ● ○ ● ○

As soon as he'd walked away, Amber was at my side. "What was that about? He knows, huh? Oh, God, does he?"

"He was just doing a little research. Wanted to know how old you are. He's definitely hooked."

I could see it in her eyes; she was going to scream. I clamped my hand over her mouth while her eyes bulged. When at last the muscles in her face relaxed, I took my hand away.

"No way!" she gasped.

"Way," I said.

"Oh, God! When is he going to ask me out again?"

"He already did, more or less."

"On a specific date, I mean! A specific time and place!"

"He will. Don't worry." My tone was a little flat, and she eyed me carefully.

"You're not happy for me."

"No, I am. It's great."

"No, you're not."

I hooked my arm in hers and started walking, so she wouldn't be able to study my face so closely. "I am, okay? Believe me. I couldn't be happier."

12:40 A.M.

Amber rang my cell a couple hours ago all hyphy.

"He messaged me! He messaged me! He messaged me!" Her voice went up an octave each time she said it, until she sounded like a soprano on helium.

"That's great."

"No, G, you don't understand. He messaged me! Rex Sands sent me, Amber, a message asking me out to dinner!"

I kicked listlessly at my bedpost. "That's cool."

"'That's cool'? What, are you deaf? It's *amazing!*"

"Uh-huh."

She paused. "What's wrong?"

"Nothing." I didn't want to get into a hugely involved discussion about the doldrums I'd been sinking into all afternoon, so I faked a little enthusiasm and added, "It's so exciting! Seriously. When do you see him?"

That was all she needed; she prattled on for a good twenty minutes, reviewing every syllable of his message, dissecting each nuance until my brain ached. Sometimes I wish I were a guy. At least their laconic, monosyllabic conversations aren't this exhausting.

After we hung up, I pulled on a hoodie, grabbed my board, and slipped out the door. There were stars poking through the navy blue sky, piercing its smooth surface like pegs in a Lite-Brite. I skated down the street, past the houses and yards, breathing in the scent of wood smoke. As I got closer to the plaza, restaurant smells perfumed the air. Here and there tourists walked hand in hand or helped each other out of gleaming BMWs, looking sleek and prosperous.

I did a U-turn away from the plaza and headed south. I wasn't in any mood for happy little vacation people. I wound back through the neighborhoods, savoring the vibration of the board under my Pumas. The night made me feel invisible. Cool air whooshed around me, pressed against my face; I carved away from the puddles cast by streetlights, melding instead with shadows, letting myself dissolve into the darkness.

I thought about skating over to Ben's house, but it was late, and I'd never just stopped by before. His parents might get weirded out. Besides, my mood was too unpredictable. Ever since my conversation with Mr. Sands today there's been this anvil in my gut that won't go away. Ben's no idiot. One look at me and he'd want to know what's up. What would I tell him? "I'm falling for our English teacher"?

I didn't even know where I was going until I'd already arrived. It embarrassed me to be there, but still I got off my board and skulked in the shadows across the street, staring at the glow of the upstairs window. He passed by once, his body just a blur of movement between the curtains. Then he was gone.

The yellow bungalow looked quaint and cheerful. Just above the balcony, as if placed there for effect, a crescent moon hung suspended in the sky. It looked exactly like a Cheshire cat's grin, tilted at a rakish angle, taunting me.

Wednesday, January 28
6:45 P.M.

When Jeremy Riggs cruised up to the Triple Shot Betty window this afternoon in a rusty old Mercury, I had to dig his name out of my memory banks. I hadn't seen him since the Floating World opening. Like most underclassmen, he's not really on my radar at school. Looking at Jeremy's big blue eyes, his nervous, uncertain mouth, I felt guilty for having forgotten him.

I slid open the window. "Hey. How's it going? Jeremy, right?"

He nodded. "I'm good. You?"

"Not bad. Hey, Amber!" I called over my shoulder. "It's Jeremy."

She sat on the counter painting her nails, totally engrossed; she spared us a quick hair-flipping look, a bland "What's up?" but beyond that she couldn't be bothered.

I turned back to him, trying not to notice the disappointment clouding his thin, pale face. "Can I get you something?"

"Oh. Um. Coffee, I guess."

"What size?"

"Small?"

I grinned. "You don't sound too sure about that."

"Actually, I just wanted to drop this off." He slipped me a CD, his tone confidential now. "Can you give this to Amber? She looks sort of busy."

"Sure."

"We're playing at the Raven this weekend. Big show."

"Oh, right!" I glanced down at the CD. He'd scribbled *Music for Amber* in little-kid handwriting. *Ohhhh!* "You guys were really good."

His voice got even quieter. "If you could talk her into coming, I'd owe you big-time."

"I'll see what I can do." I didn't want to make any promises. Amber's way too fixated on her date tomorrow night with Mr. Sands to talk about anything else.

As soon as he'd driven away, I said to her, "Look, I don't mean to be a drag here, but are you sure this thing with Mr. Sands is a good idea?"

"What?" She looked up from her nails, her eyes wide. "Are you joking?"

"It's just—this guy Jeremy worships you, and he's so cute, and talented, and he seems really nice. Maybe you should give him a chance. Just think: no more wigs, no more stress, no more trying to be something you're not."

Her jaw dropped. "I can't believe I'm hearing this."

"It's just an idea . . ."

"You think I can *decide* Rex is—what? Too much work?—and just give up on him?" She's started calling Mr. Sands "Rex." It really sort of irks me. "Is it like that for you? Like,

'Ben's kind of a hassle, I think I'll find some guy who's a little *easier*'?"

I rolled my eyes. "That's not what I meant."

"You can't back out on me." She started pacing like a caged lion in the small space, blowing on her nails impatiently. "This is too important."

"What do you mean, 'back out'?"

She turned to me, her eyes flashing. "You know what I mean. I can't pull this off without you."

I held up a hand. "Whoa. Hold up. I got the ball rolling, but from here on out I'm only a consultant. I don't get involved."

"You can't— Wait a minute!" she sputtered. "You're— like—abandoning me? Now?! When we're this close?"

"I'm not abandoning you! But—"

"But what?"

"What do you want me to do?" I challenged. "Tag along on every date and feed you lines?"

"I just want some help."

"I can't be smart for you all the time!" I blurted.

Her face went from white-hot anger to little-girl-hurt. She crumpled before my eyes. By the time the full impact of what I'd said hit me, she was out the back door, slamming it hard in my face.

"Trouble, Sloane?"

I spun around. Ben was there at the window, a sympathetic look on his face. I walked over, slid the glass all the way open. He was wearing cargo shorts and a green T-shirt. He looked cute, and seeing him there on his bike I felt a queasy wash of guilt rinse through me: guilt for subtly avoiding him since

Saturday, for thinking so much about Mr. Sands, for turning into a really shitty girlfriend and a generally despicable human being.

"Hi," I mumbled.

"Hey. Rough day?"

I nodded.

"What was all that? Something about you being smart for her?"

I bristled. "Were you eavesdropping?"

"No, I just got here and—"

"Couldn't you cough or something? Let us know you're there instead of lurking around—"

"I wasn't *lurking*." He ran his hand through his hair, his sympathy replaced now with indignation. "God, Sloane, what's up with you? You don't call, and when I stop by you bite my head off for no reason."

I grabbed a straw and started twisting it in my fingers, avoiding his eyes. "Sorry. You just startled me, is all."

For a moment, it seemed neither of us had anything to say. It was worse than arguing—that hollow, deafening silence. Finally he said, "I guess I'm going to ride over to PJ's. You free later?"

I shrugged. "Yeah. Call me."

"Actually," he said, "why don't you call me? I'm sick of leaving messages that don't get returned."

As he pedaled off down Napa Street I squinted into the sun, following him with my eyes. I hoped he might spare me a backward glance, but he didn't; he just disappeared around the corner, his graceful brown legs moving in a rhythm so practiced and assured it made me ache.

Thursday, January 29
11:15 P.M.

I didn't call Ben last night or tonight, and he didn't call me. Instead I moped around the house, restless, annoyed, and annoying. I ate like five brownies. By the time I grabbed my third, Mom offered to cancel her date with Mungo for a girls' night in. I told her she should go out and have fun. Before she left the house, though, I had to swear I wouldn't OD on chocolate.

About an hour after Mom left, Amber showed up. We hadn't exchanged a word since our stupid tiff at TSB— we'd just baristaed side by side in silence, which isn't easy when your workspace is the size of a broom closet. All day at school today we avoided each other. Since Ben didn't come find me and I wasn't about to hunt him down, I had nobody to hang out with at lunch. I gobbled my sandwich in about twenty seconds, then spent the rest of the period cowering in a shadowy corner of the library, seeking solace in *Wuthering Heights*. It sucked. Cowering in the library, I mean, not *Wuthering Heights*.

I have to admit I was glad to see Amber. She was supposed to go out to dinner with Mr. Sands tonight. She hadn't broken our silence to beg for help, which seemed like a step in the right direction—after all, we'd fought because I wanted off the hook, right? Strangely, though, knowing she'd gone out with him totally solo, no texting or anything, made me feel left out. The whole situation's messed up.

Her glum face told me things hadn't gone all that well. She stood on the doorstep staring at her shoes. She wore a thin, clingy sweater, a short denim skirt, and open-toed mules. Her hair hung down around her face and she shivered slightly in the fog.

"Hey," I said gently. "How's it going?"

In answer, she burst into tears.

I pulled her inside and got her situated on the couch while she went on crying. It was good we had the house to ourselves. I sliced an emergency-sized brownie, popped it in the microwave so the chocolate chips would soften a little, and poured her a big glass of milk.

When I returned with her prescription, her eyes lit up and the tears ebbed a bit. She took a large, medicinal bite.

"What happened?" I asked.

She knocked back some milk. A faint, ghostly mustache graced her upper lip as she answered. "I choked."

"You did not. You're too hard on yourself."

She grimaced. "No, seriously, I totally crashed and burned."

"I'll be the judge of that. Tell me what happened."

"It was awful." She put the brownie down and pushed it away. "I had like no idea what to wear, first of all. Everything I owned seemed cheap and stupid. Even the stuff Hero gave me just—eugh." She waved a hand.

"You look fine."

"Whatever. So, we agreed to meet at the restaurant. When I got there he asked if I wanted a drink, so I had to make up this whole thing about my mom being an alcoholic—actually, that's the first honest thing I've told him, really. Anyway, that's how I got around the drink thing."

"Good thinking," I said.

"Except at that point I would have given anything for a Crantini."

I nodded sympathetically. "You were nervous?"

"Nervous! I was terrified. I studied the MySpace profile you set up for me, and I really, really wanted to sound like that."

"Like what?"

She scoffed. "You know! Smart. God, if you're such a genius, how can you be so lame about some things?"

I raised an eyebrow.

She sighed. "Sorry."

"So he's there, you're there—what happened?"

"We ordered dinner, and . . ." She trailed off, staring into space.

"And . . .?"

"He wanted to talk about books. Of course." Tears started spilling over her bottom lashes and sliding down her face. "He brought up that Kerouac guy before the appetizers even came. Last night I got online and read all the Wikipedia entries about *On the Road*, I watched clips of the beats on YouTube—I learned everything I could—but it's not that easy. He knows like . . . everything . . . about everything. I know nothing."

I squeezed her knee. "You know all kinds of stuff he's got no clue about."

"Oh yeah?" Her lip trembled. "Like what?"

"Like tattoos, for example."

She rolled her eyes. "He'd find that very impressive, I'm sure."

I weighed my words carefully. "Don't be mad, but this is what I was trying to say yesterday. Hanging out with him is so much work. Wouldn't you rather date someone you can relax with?"

She looked at me for a long moment. I was afraid she'd go off again—I could see something a little like anger in her eyes—but when she spoke, her voice was even. "Geena, I don't know if you realize this, but the world I come from isn't really the world I want to stay in."

"Yeah, but you want to be yourself, don't you?"

She pulled her hair back from her face and sighed. "I don't know. I mean, who is that? I wake up every day in a filthy house that reeks of cigarettes, and I say hello to my mom's latest boyfriend, who's still in his underwear. Is that me? Does being myself mean hooking up with someone who can relate to that shit? Because I don't think I want that guy."

She kind of had a point, but there was something off about her logic too. "I'm not saying that. I just don't think love should require a complete personality transplant."

"But what if I *want* to change? What if I want to be the kind of girl Rex could fall for?"

I didn't know what to say—the truth? That she'd have to completely transform herself, redo her whole life, and become a completely different person? Not only that, but she'd have to stop being sixteen, which will happen eventually, but not in time to be very useful with Mr. Sands. She was taking this so seriously, when really it was hopeless from the start.

After a long silence, Amber seized the half-eaten brownie

and stuffed it into her mouth. When she'd swallowed, she said, "It's okay. You don't have to answer. Just because I want to be that girl doesn't mean I can. I see that."

I felt embarrassed for some reason, as if she'd read my mind. "So, how did your date end?"

She shrugged. "I made it through dinner, but he was obviously dying to get away. Afterward I walked around for like . . . I don't know, an hour?" She looked down at her feet and I saw several angry red blisters.

"Ouch."

She touched one and winced. "I can't believe I messed everything up so royally."

"You didn't." I ran a hand over her back. "It's just tough, you know? He's intimidating."

She made a sound in her throat. "You can say that again."

"I bet he'll ask you out again."

"Yeah, right." She tried to sound like she'd given up all hope, like she'd raised the white flag in surrender, but I knew by the faint glimmer in her eyes that her heart wasn't ready to call it quits. She was wounded, yes, but still she lingered dangerously in the line of fire.

"Listen, why don't you just take a little break? Don't contact him, try not to think about him so much." She opened her mouth to protest, but I stopped her. "Not forever! Just for a few days. See if anything changes. Maybe he won't seem so great if you just get a little distance."

"I don't want to stop liking him."

"You don't have to. Just take a little time to get some perspective."

She shrugged. "I guess I don't have much choice. He's not

going to ask me out anytime soon, and I can't force myself on him."

"So we agree? There's a Mr. Sands moratorium in place until Sunday?"

She nodded reluctantly. "I won't contact him, but I can't say I won't think about him."

"That's good enough for me."

Friday, January 30
2:10 P.M.

Ben's been ignoring me since Wednesday. Okay technically, he's not *ignoring* ignoring me—he says hi—but his enthusiasm is approximately one-sixtieth what it was a couple weeks ago. And yes, I admit I didn't return some of his calls earlier this week, but I was busy trying to end world hunger. Actually, I was busy writing ridiculous MySpace messages for Amber. The point is I was busy, and now Ben's totally blowing me off, which seems a little cruel and unusual.

Example: Yesterday, walking from history to English, I had to run to catch up with him. When I did, his conversation style was distinctly monosyllabic.

"Hey, stranger!" I punched his shoulder playfully, trying to keep it light. "What's going on?"

"Oh. Hi."

"You okay?"

He didn't meet my gaze. "Fine. You?"

"I'm good." I couldn't help but recall that just three weeks ago he found me irresistibly kissable between fifth and sixth period. Now he couldn't even look at me. "You just seem kind of . . ."

"What?"

"I don't know," I said. "Distant, I guess."

Before he could answer, we both spotted Sophie De Luca headed our way, her hair swinging around her shoulders with its usual shine and bounce. Actually, it wasn't just her hair that was shiny; everything about her seemed to glow. She strode toward us in a butter-colored leather blazer and perfectly cut wool trousers. Instantly I felt like a disheveled Oompa Loompa.

She fell into step beside Ben and spoke with unnecessary intimacy into his ear. "Can I borrow your notes on *The Stranger*, Benedict?"

"Sure."

"Oh, thank you so much!" She squeezed his arm affectionately. "I completely spaced out last week. Dylan—the guy I was seeing back in New York?—we broke up. It completely ruined my concentration. Relationships can be such a drag."

Apparently, it's not enough for Sophie De Luca to have everything anyone could want in life: Slavic cheekbones, mile-long legs, enough fine Italian footwear to launch a Gucci empire. No, now she's got to invade my turf, crowning herself Queen Bee and turning Ben into one of her drones.

I hoped Ben would pointedly turn his attention back to me, his girlfriend. Instead, he offered her a sympathetic smile. "That's good you've got such a healthy attitude."

"Well, you know, *c'est la vie, carpe diem*—"

"*Que sera, sera*," I added, my tone nastier than I'd intended.

They both looked at me like I'd just sprouted horns or something.

"Hey," Sophie said, her tone going from bubbly to snide. "What's up with your friend Amber?"

"I don't know what you're talking about," I said dismissively.

By then we'd reached the classroom. Mr. Sands sat grading papers behind his desk. I cast a nervous glance at him, not liking where this was going.

"Hello! She's always got some weird wig on these days. I just saw her in the bathroom wearing a horrible blond thing—it looked *so* not sanitary."

"Unsanitary," I mumbled.

"What?"

Ben, handing his notes to Sophie, said, "Why *is* she wearing wigs lately?"

He's supposed to be my boyfriend, and he's siding with Sophie De Luca in my hour of need? I looked from one to the other in mute horror.

Praise God, the bell rang just then, saving me from their queries. Mr. Sands put his pen down, stood up, and we all shuffled off to our seats like good little AP robots.

Now here I sit in my uncomfortable desk, listening to Mr. Sands go on about Camus. My journal is artfully concealed inside my binder, and I look up now and then with an engrossed nod so Mr. Sands will assume I'm jotting down his every word. Normally this posture is authentic—I really do write down everything he says—but now I'm too distracted. I can feel all these questions hatching in my brain. Namely:

1) How long can Amber keep up her bizarre little charade?

2) Is Ben actually my boyfriend anymore?

3) If I didn't like it when he kissed me in the hallway, do I like it better now that he ignores me to provide spontaneous relationship counseling for Sophie De Luca?

4) Is he going to ask me to the Valentine's dance, or will he ask Sophie?

5) If my mind launches off into rapid-fire fantasyland whenever Mr. Sands calls on me, or looks at me, or turns to write something on the board, does this mean I'm cheating on Ben inside my brain?

6) Can I really cheat on Ben if he's barely even talking to me?

7) If I pluck my eyebrows just right, will they look like Sophie's?

Saturday, January 31
3:30 P.M.

Amber came into work today wearing a ragged, torn sweatshirt and stretched-out sweats. She also had on black lipstick—a sure sign she's harboring death-rocker ennui.

"What's up with you?" I asked. "Channeling Marilyn Manson?"

"Men suck." She tossed her bag on the counter and pulled out her sketchbook.

"Oh-kay."

She glared at me accusingly. "He hasn't messaged me—obviously."

"I figured."

"Oh, you 'figured.' What does that mean?"

"Um, Amber? We're not talking about this, remember?"
She groaned.

"Everyone knows the best way to get over someone is to
think about someone else." See, I have a new plan—or rather,
an old plan taken up a notch. I'm determined to convince
Amber that Jeremy Riggs is hot. Well, if not hot, at least
intriguing. I'm sure once she sees how much fun it is to be
with someone who's not, well, totally wrong for her in every
way, she'll toss Mr. Sands aside and fall for Jeremy—someone
who likes the real Amber, not some fake intellectual she's
busting her butt to become.

I powered up the ancient boom box we keep on the
shelf above the Italian syrups and stuck Jeremy's CD in. I
still hadn't given it to her, despite my promise. I knew if I
simply handed it over it'd just end up on the floorboards of
her mom's filthy El Dorado, so I had to trick her into listening
and hopefully liking it. If I could just distract her from this
Mr. Sands fixation, I knew our lives would get easier. I pushed
PLAY and, after a brief pause, Jeremy's voice filled Triple Shot
Betty, startling us both.

"Listen, Amber, I'm incredibly shy and not very good at
talking to—well, human beings in general—but I can express
myself through music, for some reason, even if I do it badly
sometimes. I write way too many songs, and lately every song
I write seems to be about you. Here are a few I put together.
It's me on guitar, me on bass, me on everything, actually. So
yeah, this is what I call the *Amber Collection.*"

The first song started up. The sound had a different flavor

from the Aqua Nets; this was quirkier, more poetic, sort of Death-Cab-for-Cutie-meets-the-Magnetic-Fields. I liked it a lot.

"Oh my God," I gushed, grabbing the jewel case and pulling out the scribbled song list. "It's so romantic! He's got like seven songs on here. 'Tattoo Diva,' 'Stock Boy Soliloquy,' 'Ode to a Triple Shot Betty.' This is like a John Hughes movie!"

"Let's not overreact," she said, but I could see the intrigue in her eyes. "Jeremy gave this to you?"

"Yeah. Wednesday."

"Wednesday? And I'm just now hearing about it?"

"Yeah."

"Why?"

I gave her a look. "Let's just say you were preoccupied."

She started to say something, paused to listen as he segued into the second verse, and finally asked, "Wait a minute—why did he give it to you?"

I shrugged. "You were busy painting your nails."

We stood there and let his surprisingly deep voice wash over us; he was hitting the chorus now, gaining momentum. *I want to be the sugar in your coffee, I want to be the honey in your tea, you've got enough attitude for both of us, can't you turn your attitude on me?*

I laughed. "He's got you pegged."

Amber tried not to smile but failed. "Shut up."

Jeremy, the little emo-kid-who-could, had her attention at last. I wanted to do a victory dance, but I knew if I pulled out *I told you so* too soon, she'd go on ignoring him just to be perverse.

"What are you going to do?" I squeezed her hands, squelching the urge to jump up and down. "You have to respond—the poor guy! He's dying to know what you think. He's dying!"

She bit her lip. "No wonder he was so weird at work yesterday."

"Romeo of the tattoo parlor. Oh, *swoon!*"

She slapped my arm. "*You* date him if he's so cool."

"He doesn't want me. He wants you. And bad!" I put on my I-just-got-a-brilliant-idea face, even though I'd worked out this plan hours before. "Hey! He's playing at the Raven tonight in Healdsburg. We should totally go!"

"Really? You want to?" She looked excited for a second, but then her face fell. "I can't get the car, though. Could Ben drive us?"

It was my turn to frown. Since Ben and I are barely speaking, I didn't feel like asking a favor.

She must have read my expression, because she asked, "What's up with you guys, anyway?"

"We're kind of not talking."

"What? How did that happen? Why didn't you tell me?"

"It's not that big a deal. I don't think." I started chewing on the end of my braid. It's gross, but it helps me when I get freaked out, and it's better than eating your fingernails. "He told me he messed around with Sophie last year."

"Before you got together?"

I nodded.

"So, what's the problem?"

"I feel weird about it."

"It's not like he cheated on you. Mocha?"

I nodded, and she started brewing us a couple shots.

"It's weird when you get involved with someone, you know?" I started arranging the paper cups into neat little rows. "Like sex starts to take over everything."

She spun around. "You had sex?"

"No! I just mean—you know—messing around. Sometimes I feel like he's more interested in my body than my brain."

She snorted. "Wish I could get Rex to stop probing my brain and start noticing my body."

I shot her a look. "One word: moratorium."

"I know, I know. Anyway, you guys aren't breaking up, are you?"

"I don't think so." I gave up on the cups and went back to my braid. "But how am I supposed to know? I've never had a boyfriend before."

Just then I heard the distinct cough of a decrepit old Volvo, and my heart leaped into my throat. Ben!

It wasn't, though. It was the other ancient Volvo driver in my life, the one I didn't choose but still have to deal with: Mungo.

"Good morning," he called in his thick accent. He looked all soccer coachy in a bright yellow Windbreaker and blue baseball cap. "How, are you, Geena? Hi, Amber! Having a good weekend?"

Okay, about Mungo: He's really nice. I mean, he's so nice that it's almost impossible to dislike him. I generally disappear into my room when he comes over, but I can already tell that hating him isn't an option. That accent alone makes you grin, even if you're dead set on being surly. Still, just because he's preternaturally likeable doesn't mean I have to welcome him into the family with open arms or anything, right?

"Hey, Mungo," I said. "What can I get you?"

"What's your mum's favorite coffee drink, do you know?"

"Probably a soy latte. You want one of those?"

He smiled, all starry eyed, as if just thinking about her favorite beverage made him giddy. "Please. And a double cappuccino. Can't seem to wake up this morning."

"Because he's been so *busy* every night," Amber mumbled into my ear.

I made a face at her and shoved her toward the espresso machine.

"What size on those?" I tried very hard not to think about this man—or anyone—having sex with my parental unit. Gag.

"Medium, I guess."

While Amber brewed his drinks, I attempted small talk. It's awkward, though. I don't know him any better than the millions of other random people who drive up to my window in search of a fix. Yet in his case, we both know we could end up living together someday—maybe even exchanging Christmas gifts and going on road trips. That's just weird.

"What are you and Mom up to this weekend?" I asked.

"Taking her to dinner tonight. There's a new place in Healdsburg—supposed to be very good. Tomorrow we might go for—"

"Wait, did you say Healdsburg?"

He nodded. "There was a review in the PD. Did you see

it? They gave this little bistro five stars. I thought your mum might fancy it."

Amber and I exchanged are-you-thinking-what-I'm-thinking looks. It wasn't ideal, getting ferried to a show with the geriatric set, but it sure beat not going at all. I turned back to Mungo. "You think we could get a ride? There's a band we want to see at the Raven."

I swear, his face lit up like a Christmas tree. "Sure." He patted his car affectionately. "Old Bessie here's got plenty of room. Who will it be then? You and Ben?"

"No." I suddenly missed Ben something terrible. "Amber and me."

Amber came over with his drinks, all charm and steaming cups. She put lids on them carefully and handed them over. "That would be great if we could hitch a ride."

"No problem!" He took the drinks from her and handed me a ten. "Keep the change. See you girls tonight."

"Big tipper!" Amber said approvingly "Your 'mum' has decent taste."

"Yeah," I said. "He seems pretty cool."

"You don't sound that happy about it."

I shrugged. "Could be worse. At least we get to see the Aqua Nets tonight."

Jeremy's CD was still playing, and Amber bobbed her head to the bass beat. For now, that was all the encouragement I required. Phase One of Operation Forget Rex has officially begun.

Sunday, February 1

2:00 A.M.

How am I supposed to get Amber off crack when the crack shows up everywhere? Really, how annoying is that? We'd been at the Raven for like five minutes when guess who walked in the door? You got it: Mr. Sands.

Operation Forget Rex went from All Systems Go to *Abort! Abort!* in record time.

Okay, on the semi-bright side, he wasn't alone. This was good in that it forced Amber to keep her distance, but bad in terms of my master plan. Nothing sends a girl's obsessive instincts into overdrive like spotting said obsession with another girl. In this case, the other "girl" came as a total shock to both of us.

Mr. Sands was on a date. With Ms. Boyle.

Ms. Boyle, our history teacher! Ms. Boyle, who's at least thirty, never wears a bra, and is famous for her hairy armpits, which make their debut each spring in sleeveless blouses and continue to haunt the classroom until summer. Ms. Boyle, whose walls are plastered with posters of Malcolm X and Bob Dylan and huge handmade banners on recycled paper with Day-Glo letters screaming slogans like BE THE CHANGE YOU WANT TO SEE IN THE WORLD! That Ms. Boyle.

How had this happened?

In a funny way (not funny like ha-ha, but funny like twisted) I felt just as spurned as Amber—maybe more so.

By showing up with Ms. Boyle on his arm, Mr. Sands was apparently saying he'd take this frizzy-haired neo-hippie over us. After all we'd done to woo him, all our slaving away on MySpace and reading his favorite books, how could he just leave us in the dust for a woman who's about as sexy as a slab of tofu?

"There they are." Amber poked my side for like the thousandth time. "My God, what is she *wearing*?"

"Stop looking!" I hollered over the music. "You're being way too obvious."

Instead of gazing adoringly at Jeremy working the frets of his Stratocaster, Amber kept craning her neck to catch sight of Mr. Sands and Ms. Boyle. I'll admit, I gave in to the urge to peek a few times myself. They showed no signs of spotting us the whole night. In a last-ditch effort to resurrect my original purpose, I tried to shift Amber's attention away from their date-in-progress and back up onto the stage.

"Jeremy just looked at you when he sang that line! Did you see that? He looked right at you."

"He just put his hand on her waist." Predictably, she ignored my efforts entirely. "Gross!"

Basically, our conversation turned into a series of non sequiturs.

"That song was so sweet," I'd say. "You think Jeremy wrote that one?"

"Oh, God," she'd reply, "look at her hair. You think she's ever heard of conditioner?"

"Jeremy looks so cute tonight. I love that little streak of blue in his bangs."

"She's a vegetarian. You can tell just by looking at her."

"Amber! Jeremy just smiled right at you!"

"How can he even *think* about kissing her? She's got no lips!"

You get the picture.

By the time we caught a ride with Mom and Mungo back to Sonoma, I was exhausted, Amber was depressed, and Operation Forget Rex was in tatters. We filled the backseat of Mungo's Volvo with an acrid silence.

"What's the matter?" Mom asked, twisting around in the passenger seat to survey our glum expressions. "Wasn't the band any good?"

"They were great." Even I could tell my tone was more suited to a funeral than a concert.

"So what's the problem?" She looked concerned.

"No problem."

"What about you, Amber?" Mom persisted. "Did you have fun?"

Amber kept her gaze out the window. "Yeah," she said flatly. "A blast."

"Was it that 'emo' music, then?" Mungo asked brightly, studying us in the rearview mirror.

"What's that got to do with anything?" It came out snippier than I meant it to.

"'Emo' is quite gloomy, right?"

"Sort of," I said. "I guess."

"Well, then, you're just getting into the mood of it, right?" He turned to Mom. "I read about it in *Newsweek*."

Mom looked suitably impressed at how hip her date was.

Meanwhile, Amber and I slipped into an ever deeper funk in the backseat.

3:00 P.M.

Amber and I started the morning shift at TSB today in grumpy, morose silence. I tried to cheer her up by popping Jeremy's CD into the player, but I think it just reminded us both of the hideous Boyle-and-Sands sighting last night.

"Maybe they're a good couple." It was useless to bring up anything else, so I decided we might as well talk about it.

Amber scoffed. "How do you figure?"

"They're both like . . . anachronistic."

"In English, please?"

"Sorry. SAT word. They're both stuck in another time. Ms. Boyle's all into the sixties and Mr. Sands is more like the fifties."

"Rex is nothing like her. She's an anemic string bean with bad hair."

"I agree, they're not well matched in terms of attractiveness."

"Plus she's way too old for him!"

"Amber, the age difference between them is less than you and him."

"So? The older woman thing never works out." She folded her arms. "She'll just feel dried up and ancient. Correction: *more* dried up and ancient than she already is. You see it all the time in *People*."

We both heard the growl of that distinctive old motor simultaneously, and we turned to the window as one. Oh, God, just when I'm trying to get her off the junk, her drug of choice shows up again. Mr. Sands grinned lazily from behind the wheel of his MG, mirrored sunglasses confronting us with our shocked faces in miniature.

"Turn it off," Amber ordered, nodding at the boom box.

Reluctantly, I did as I was told.

"Hey," she said quietly. "What's up?"

I tried to look busy wiping down the espresso machine, but I couldn't keep from eavesdropping even if I tried.

"Gorgeous day, huh?" I heard him say.

It was a gorgeous day—I had to give him that. The sun hadn't yet climbed higher than the treetops, but already you could see it would be one of those freakishly beautiful winter days in Sonoma County, when the hills are bright green and everything—the houses, the oaks, even the curls of morning fog—are luminous with the promise of spring.

"Yeah," Amber said. "Pretty."

"I'm thinking about going for a drive later—maybe check out Glen Ellen, see Jack London's house." He propped his sunglasses up onto his head.

"He a friend of yours?"

I cringed. Oh, God. They went together like aged scotch and Spam.

Mr. Sands hesitated, then let out a wry chuckle. "Yeah, Amber, he's a friend of mine. God, you're so deadpan sometimes, you kill me."

Amber just giggled uneasily.

Mr. Sands glanced at me. "Geena, could I get a double latte?"

"Sure." I was grateful for something to do, though I didn't want to miss their conversation while I steamed the milk.

"I read your blog." He dropped his volume slightly. I

edged a little closer as I measured out the espresso. One night last week when I couldn't sleep, I posted an old paper I wrote about *Wuthering Heights* to Amber's MySpace page. It was stupid, I know, but I wanted Mr. Sands to read it. I needed to know if it was as brilliant as I thought it was. "Okay, don't laugh, but I've read it seven times. You're really a good writer."

My heart thundered. He spoke to Amber, but his words sailed through her to me. My blog! He'd read it seven times! I saw him in the dead of night, flipping on a bedside lamp, booting up his laptop to read it one more time. He'd sucked meaning from my syntax, whispered whole sentences aloud so he could taste each syllable on his tongue. The intimacy gave me goose bumps.

"Extraordinary intelligence paired with razor-sharp wit. That's a very dangerous combination." His voice dipped low, confiding; it went husky around the edges.

I felt seriously dizzy, as if our tiny espresso shack had transformed into an elevator. I gripped the steam wand for stability.

"I'm glad you think so," Amber returned.

"You made me see Heathcliff in a new light."

"Ha," Amber said. "Yeah. Well."

I had to steam his milk then—there was no getting around it. I did it as quickly as possible so as not to miss a single word about my writing or Heathcliff or anything else. By the time I'd finished, though, they weren't saying anything, just smiling at each other, their eyes locked, messages firing back and forth between them with rapid-fire intensity.

"Double latte," I said, handing it out the window to him.

He still didn't stop staring at Amber as he took it from me and handed over a five. I got him his change. Any happiness his compliments had stirred now turned to dust inside me. Their dreamy staring contest made me feel like a gnat buzzing just beyond their field of vision.

Finally he slipped his sunglasses back on and put the car into gear. "Call me sometime."

"Okay." The word came out sort of strangled, like she couldn't quite get enough air in her lungs.

As he drove off I made a point of not looking at her; I cleaned the espresso machine with an attention to detail I usually lack.

Amber erupted in a quick, explosive scream that set my teeth on edge.

"Do you have to do that?" I turned toward her, holding up a hand as if that could shield me from the sound.

"Did you hear that? Oh my God!"

I nodded. "Yeah, that's great."

"He likes me, G! He really, really likes me."

Okay, I could have pointed out that he liked her blog, which was written by me. I could have reminded her that just last night we'd seen him with Ms. Boyle. I could have said any number of things that would have killed her buzz, but I didn't. All I said was, "Yeah."

Inside, though, I was thinking, *When will this madness end?*

Monday, February 2
11:10 P.M.

To: herolovespink@gmail.com
From: skatergirl@yahoo.com
Subject: Confuse-o-Rama

Hero,
Okay, so far, February is looking sketchy at best. Ben's
ignoring me, Amber's still obsessed with Mr. Sands, and I'm
terminally confused. Ever since Ben told me he and Sophie
messed around, things have been off kilter. You know what
I mean? It's like a little wedge has been driven between us—
just a splinter, really, but I think it might be getting infected.
Instead of figuring out how to fix it, though, I get more and
more distracted by this zany situation with Amber and
Mr. Sands. It's so hopeless. I try to convince her to focus
on someone else—namely, the adorable sophomore who's
insanely in love with her—but every time I try to help, I
end up more confused.

Geena

To: skatergirl@yahoo.com
From: herolovespink@gmail.com
Subject: RE: Confuse-o-Rama

Geebs,
Ben's ignoring you? Come on Cuz, this is me you're talking
to. Ben wouldn't do that unless you'd given him plenty of

reason to. I'm not trying to be disloyal, I'm just pointing out that occasionally you can be a little pigheaded and you don't always notice the signals you're sending. Think back: Did you offend him? And what's all this about Sophie? Are you punishing him for a little dalliance that happened before he was even your boyfriend? That hardly seems fair.

I know this might come off as harsh, G, and I don't mean it that way. I'd just hate to see you screw things up with Ben. Be honest with yourself and with him. Try not to let your boy-hostile tendencies win out over common sense.

Kisses,
Hero

Tuesday, February 3

7:20 P.M.

Gods of Tuesday, I bow down to your glory! Also, special thanks to the gods of Volvos, the gods of Cheetos, and the gods of February rain.

Today started out sucky but turned out fabu. Throughout all our classes, Ben stuck to his lukewarm routine. His ability to ignore me without totally ignoring me was astounding. By the time the final bell rang, I knew I couldn't take it another second. I marched over to his locker and stood there with my hands on my hips. He just kept on loading books into his messenger bag, which infuriated me.

"What's going on? Why are you acting like I don't exist?" Sure, I may have started this ignoring-each-other trend on accident, but that didn't mean I had to put up with constant neglect, did it?

He turned to me, surprised. "Sorry?"

"Don't give me that look."

"What look?"

"Like you've got no idea what I'm talking about," I sneered. *You* know and *I* know that you've been ignoring me. I just want to understand why."

Sophie sauntered over to her locker just then and smiled at Ben sympathetically.

"And you," I said to her, shocked at my own assertiveness, "can stop grinning like that, okay?"

"Well, excuse me." She flicked her eyes to Ben. "I didn't realize happiness was a crime."

"Happiness isn't the problem. It's your smugness I take issue with."

Ben slammed his locker shut, slung his bag over his shoulder, and guided me away from Sophie firmly. I thrummed under his touch; the combination of adrenaline and his arm around my shoulder made for a potent, fizzy cocktail in my bloodstream.

"You have your stuff?" Ben asked.

"Uh—my—?" I stammered.

"You need anything from your locker?"

"No. I'm good."

He guided me out to the parking lot, never removing his arm from my shoulder. There was something so confident about the way he led me to his car. A part of me felt intimidated, but mostly it was just sexy.

He opened the passenger door for me, slammed it once I'd gotten in, then climbed into the driver's seat. Then he put the car into gear and tore out of the parking lot before the intersection could get all congested with other eager escapees.

"Uh, where are we going?"

"Anywhere. I don't care. We need to talk."

We drove north in silence. When the houses thinned out he took a side road west through the vineyards. Finally he pulled over, and we found ourselves staring out the windshield at a small cottage surrounded by rows and rows of spindly, bare vines. A gentle rain started pattering on the roof of his Volvo. He turned off the motor and we just listened to the rhythm of the drops.

"I've been ignoring you because you've been ignoring me."

I shot him a surprised glance. "Really? I started this?"

"Don't pretend you don't know that, Sloane! You and Amber are so caught up in your own little world, it's like I don't even exist."

"She sort of needed my help," I said, staring at my lap.

"With what? What was so important that you had to stop returning my calls?" A muscle in his jaw pulsed. He looked mad.

I couldn't tell him about Mr. Sands, obviously. "She's just been kind of high-maintenance lately." That sounded weak, even to me.

"If you don't want to be with me, just say so."

"I do—I—want to—but—"

"Real convincing there, Sloane." He gripped the steering wheel and stared straight ahead.

"No, listen—I'm serious! I want to be with you."

"Then why do I get the feeling you don't?"

"Because I'm not used to this!"

He looked at me. "Not used to what?"

"To being a . . . girlfriend."

"You say it like it's a disease." His expression softened a little—the trace of a smile tugged at his mouth, though he resisted.

"I've never been with anyone," I told him. "It's all new to me."

"So are you saying you're not ready for a relationship?"

"No. I'm ready. I think I'm ready now. Maybe I wasn't before." I paused. "I miss you."

He seemed about to reach for me, but he stopped himself, as if remembering something.

"What?" I asked. "What are you thinking?"

He studied me. "Does this have anything to do with what I told you about me and Sophie?"

Just hearing him say her name made me feel a little sick. I didn't want to think about her right now. "I don't know. Maybe."

He leaned slightly toward me, making me look him in the eye. "I'm not interested in her like that. You know that, right?"

Did I know that? Not really. It's pretty hard to believe. I mean, she's everything I'm not: sophisticated, smooth, gorgeous. How could Ben not be tempted? "You really don't want to be with her?"

"Of course not." He brushed a strand of hair away from my face. "I want to be with you."

"You don't have to say that just to make me feel bet—"

"Geena!" He looked incredulous. "Come on. I wouldn't lie to you."

I looked down again. "Then I guess I'll have to believe you."

"Something's going on with you, Sloane. Why don't you just tell me?"

My head whirred like a swarm of locusts were trapped in there. Should I go into this whole crazy situation with Mr. Sands? What would I say? "I've been busy trying to seduce our English teacher"? Telling him that would just be humiliating. It's not like Mr. Sands could ever be a real threat, since Ben is an actual person, someone I'm involved with, and Mr. Sands is more like, I don't know, Johnny Depp or something. Then again, if I have feelings for Mr. Sands and don't tell him, how can I resent him for secretly crushing on Sophie?

"It's complicated," I said.

"Just try."

I took a deep breath. "I'm trying to figure out how to be with you but not let that overshadow everything else." Pathetic, generic, incredibly vague, fairly off topic, but not a total lie, at least.

"Okay," he said, obviously still mystified.

"I'm not explaining myself very well."

"No, no," he said, "I think I get that. Like you still want to be friends with Amber and keep up your grades and stuff, right?"

I just nodded.

"I want that too." His eyes sparkled. "I mean, no way am I giving up my spot as valedictorian just because I'm into you."

"Salutatorian, you mean." I smiled. And then, seeing as we were having a moment and I was terrified my horrible-at-poker-face would give something away, I leaned over and kissed him. The heat of his response surprised me. Suddenly his hands were everywhere. I felt his fingers tangle in my hair and I let out a low, barely audible moan and our bodies just sort of found each other, like that was what they wanted all along. Within seconds, the windows of the Volvo were steamed up and I was basically in his lap.

"Whoa," I breathed, pulling back a bit. He had my bra undone, somehow (who knew Ben could be so smooth?) and all at once I felt way too exposed. "Maybe we should slow down."

For a second, he looked so disappointed, I almost wanted to take it back. Then I thought, *Wait a second, am I turning into one of those girls who has sex just because she's desperate to please some guy?* That seemed really pathetic. I reached under my shirt and fastened my bra, feeling awkward and gawky as I scooted back over to my seat.

He sat back, his eyes filled with a strange mix of confusion and desire. "I'm sorry, Geena."

"No, don't be."

"Listen, I want to ask you something, and maybe this isn't the right time, but . . ." He paused.

"What?"

"Will you go to the Valentine's dance with me?"

"The Valentine's dance?" I echoed stupidly.

"Yeah—I know you probably think it's lame, but do you want to go?"

I laughed. "Yeah. Let's do it. Why not?"

"Cool."

I nodded. "Excellent."

The smooth, beautiful skin of his neck called to me. I wanted to touch him again. I leaned over and trailed kisses from his jaw to the collar of his T-shirt.

He pulled back and raised an eyebrow. "You're one confusing chick—you know that?"

"I prefer 'Woman of Mystery.'"

"Yeah." He laughed. "I can see why."

We stayed in the car, laughing and talking for over two hours. Things got sort of hot again once or twice, but we never moved to the backseat. I was starving, and Ben found half a bag of Cheetos for us to devour. Big, fat drops splattered against the tinny roof of the Volvo, tapping out a rhythm I can only describe as euphoric. The Cheetos turned our fingers a neon orange and later, when I kissed him good-bye, I could taste the salty seasoning on his lips.

Who knew imitation Cheddar could be so divine?

Wednesday, February 4

7:00 P.M.

Ben and I studied for our French test together at the library after school. We sat at a table behind the Norse Mythology section. Since nobody needed any books about Valhalla or Valkyries, we pretty much had that corner to ourselves. We worked out a stupid little game we called *"Embrassez-moi."* Basically we tested each other with flashcards, and when one of us got ten words in a row without a single mistake, the quizzer had to reward the quizzee with a kiss. It was juvenile, yes, but still fun. The kisses seemed to get hotter and hotter. What is it about libraries that amplifies the sexual tension so effectively?

When I got home I was in a pretty good mood, really.

Then I walked into the kitchen and found my mom and Mungo on the floor.

I did what any sane person would do when confronted with two middle-aged people in the throes of passion, one of whom is said sane person's mother: I screamed.

"Geena!" Mom sat up quickly, struggling to straighten out her clothes. "Jesus."

It's not like they were naked or anything—I'd be hospitalized now if I'd had to deal with that trauma. Still, they were going at it in a way that nobody wants exposure to.

Mungo turned the color of a stewed tomato. "Right. Well. Sorry about that."

They both got to their feet with as much dignity as they could muster (i.e., none).

I shook my head like someone waking from a nightmare. "Okay, let's get one thing straight: This will never happen again." Mom opened her mouth to say something, but nothing came out.

"I'm serious." I have no idea where this came from, but I was bristling with righteous indignation. "I live here too, and you guys have to respect that."

"We do." Mom brushed a bit of lint off her pants. "Of course we do, honey. I just wasn't—"

"Thinking," I finished. "You weren't thinking because you're so into him. Believe it or not there are other people on the planet, though, one of whom happens to be your daughter. Don't let it happen again."

Then I stormed off to my room.

I seriously don't know what that was all about. It just flew out of my mouth.

7:50 P.M.

After Mungo left, Mom came into my room and sat down on the edge of my bed. She waited until I looked up, then asked me very quietly, "You okay?"

"Fine."

"That was embarrassing. I'm sorry."

I just shrugged. All of my moral indignation had vanished. I was left feeling tired and a little sheepish. Also, I was hungry, but I'd been afraid to venture out into the kitchen again.

"Geena, I really like him. You know that, right?"

I nodded.

"I think I might even be in love with him."

This was skirting the edge of too much information, but I resisted the urge to cover my ears and go "Nah-nah-nah-nah-nah!" Instead I said, "That's good. Right?"

She smiled sadly. "Yeah. It's great."

"So why do you say it like that?"

"Like what?"

"Like it depresses you."

"Well . . ." She hugged her knees. "It's complicated. I've been pretty lonely since your dad and I split up. Mungo's the first person to come along that I can see myself with."

She paused, her eyes searching the ceiling. My mind raced ahead. God, they weren't getting married already, were they? Was she going to have another kid? I thought of this girl I know, Jana Clark. Her mom had a baby in September and after that Jana would show up at football games with her baby sister in a stroller, showing her off like she was a new iPod or something. I thought it was pretty tacky. I had no desire for a baby sibling accessory. Besides, our house is really small. How are we going to fit Mungo and a screaming infant in here while I'm studying for the SATs? Talk about bad timing.

"Are you pregnant?" As soon it was out of my mouth, I knew it sounded totally ridiculous and accusatory.

"No! Of course not. Nothing like that." She smoothed my hair. "Don't be silly. I wouldn't do that to you."

I shook my head. "Sorry. I don't know where that came from."

"It's a big deal, having a guy around. You barely know him." She lifted my chin with her finger so I had to look right at her. "You're still the most important, though, okay? No matter what happens with Mungo. You're always most important. Don't ever forget that."

Okay, this was getting a little Lifetime movie cheese ball for me, but I could feel my throat closing up with emotion anyway. I just nodded, afraid that if I tried to speak, it would come out all quivery and then the violins would really kick in.

She kissed me on the forehead and got up to leave.

"Anything to eat?" I asked.

She paused at the door. "I think there's some leftover pizza."

"I know it's a foreign concept, but most moms *cook* in the kitchen."

"Ha, ha," she said.

Thursday, February 5

4:15 P.M.

This morning as I turned in my French test I decided *"Embrassez-moi"* was pretty brilliant, really. The exam was horrendously difficult, but I was confident I'd aced it. I was wondering if the same technique would work with trig, my worst subject. Ben hadn't quite finished, so I was waiting for him in the hall. He emerged looking tired but triumphant. Without warning he leaned over and bit me on the neck. I laughed, pushing him away.

"Avez-vous bien fait sur l'épreuve?" I asked.

"Évidemment! Je recevrai une meilleure qualité que vous, sans doute."

I scoffed. Before I could think up a witty Franco-friendly reply, though, Sophie swooshed out of the classroom and strode right over to us in a cloud of expensive perfume. Coincidentally, she looked quite French today in a blue and white striped sweater and a flippy little navy blue skirt—trés chic. As usual, I felt hideously unfashionable and uncultured compared to her.

"Hey, guys!"

Ben smiled at her. "Bonjour!"

"Hi," I mumbled.

"I've been meaning to tell you, I'm having some people over after the dance next Saturday," she said. "Our house on the coast isn't rented that weekend. You two want to come? It's not like a party or anything, just a small group. My folks will be in New York."

Ben looked at me, then at her. "Maybe."

"We can stay there that night and hang out on the beach Sunday."

"Who's going?" Ben asked, sneaking another look at me. I could tell he wanted to gauge my reaction. I could also tell he wanted to go. I thought it sounded like a nightmare, for obvious reasons, but I didn't want him to know that. Clearly, this would be the after-party, even if it was billed as a casual gathering. Monday morning, the elite few who were at the De Lucas' place would be the envy of everyone. What kind of petty girl keeps her boyfriend from such a perfect weekend just because the invitation comes from her stunning, bitchy rival?

"PJ and I are going to the dance—as friends, of course. His girlfriend is studying abroad," Sophie said. "So it'll be me, PJ, you guys, maybe two other couples. There are five bedrooms, so we can ask a few more people if we want."

My mom would never go for that. An overnight out of town with guys and no adults? She'd freak.

"Everything okay, Geena?" Sophie's icy blue eyes studied me intently.

"Huh? Yeah. Why?"

"You just look a little worried. Did you have other plans?" She tossed her hair over one shoulder in that alpha-female way. Was it my imagination, or was her question edged with a barely veiled snarkiness?

"Oh, no. Not really."

"You think your parents would give you trouble? Ben's folks would be fine with it, since our families are friends, but maybe your mom wouldn't approve . . . ?"

Okay, definite snarkieness detected this time, no imagination required. And damn my perpetually naked face! Why do I have to telegraph every single thought that ever crosses my mind? I'm hopeless.

Ben stepped in. "I could talk to your mom. I mean, if you want to go, that is."

Oh, great! Put me on the spot, why don't you? You two are just so chummy with your Tahoe adventures and coastal getaways. If it weren't for me, you could go flitting about the state unhindered. I hated that I was the one with hang-ups, the one with an old-fashioned mother and old-fashioned rules. I felt so childish next to them.

"I'm sure she'll be fine with it," I said in a rush.

They both looked at me with raised eyebrows. What did Sophie know about my mom, anyway? Had Ben been talking about my family to her? Do they laugh behind my back about how babyish I am?

"Sloane, really, I could talk to her—" Ben began.

"It's not a big deal!" I snapped.

Ben took half a step back, startled. Sophie looked right at me and smirked. An unreasonable anger welled up inside me when I saw her expression. I've never really wanted to hit someone before, but right then the idea of slapping that look off her face was almost irresistible.

Thank God, the third-period late bell rang, saving me from my violent impulse.

What am I going to do about this nightmarish weekend getaway, though? Now I have to go. How can I not? Of course, going will mean being grounded for the rest of my natural life.

Great. This Valentine's Day thing is sure working out well.

Friday, February 6
11:45 P.M.

Dad was in town for a couple days meeting with some clients, so he picked me up around six and we went out for pizza, then caught a movie downtown. He and Mungo exchanged niceties in the kitchen for a torturous ten minutes. Mom was in the shower, so she was spared the agony, but I had to sit there digging at the grout on the counter while they reminded each other how civilized they are, how they don't mind at all that they've slept with the same woman, since they're both such modern, progressive, open-minded guys.

The whole experience was time suckage defined, so I was completely ecstatic when we finally escaped. Sitting across from Dad, wolfing down an extra-large pepperoni pizza forty minutes later, though, I could tell by the way he looked around the restaurant nervously and scratched his earlobe every five seconds that the awkwardness wasn't over yet.

"So, uh, looks like Jen is moving in." He announced this in the same tone normal people might say "Looks like it's going to rain."

I stopped chewing and just stared at him.

"Well, it only makes sense. Rent in Santa Monica is astronomical, and I've got a big place—not huge, but, you know."

"Actually, I don't know. I've never been down there,

remember?" Okay, this was below the belt, yeah, but come on! Jen is the epitome of a midlife crisis mistake. Now he was telling me they were taking their sad little relationship to the next level?

"Well, you should visit. Maybe over spring break."

Yeah, right! Now that the Bimbomeister is in residence, visiting him sounds majorly sucky.

"Geena, don't look at me like that."

"Like what?"

He scratched his earlobe again. "Like you want me to feel guilty."

"Can I ask you something?" I put my pizza down. The gooey cheese and glistening meat didn't look nearly as appetizing as it had two minutes ago.

"Sure."

"What does Jen have that Mom doesn't?"

He sighed. "Your mom and I were very happy for many years, Geena. Sometimes, though, something happens and you stop being good for each other."

"Why, though? What happened?"

He balled up his napkin and squinted at the far wall. I tried to be patient. He wasn't just blowing me off, I could see that, and I really wanted to know the answer. When he finally spoke, his voice was quiet but concentrated, like someone telling a secret.

"At first we brought out the best in each other. After a while, though, we started seeing all the flaws—to the point where we couldn't even see what we loved anymore. We made each other feel small. That's just not good. If you can't turn that around, there's no point in staying together."

I looked at my lap. "And Jen makes you feel big again?"

He exhaled a little laugh. "Sort of. I guess you could say that. Jen and I see the good in each other. I feel strong when I'm with her—strong and happy."

"But won't you end up seeing her flaws eventually? Won't she see yours?"

"Maybe." He shrugged. "That's the gamble, I guess."

Now, staring at my ceiling, I can't help but wonder what to do with this information. I mean, if love is all about how someone makes you see yourself, where does that put Ben and me? Sometimes he makes me feel unbearably alive and expansive, like a supernova exploding in all directions. Other times, though—especially when Sophie's in the picture—I feel like gum on the sole of someone's shoe.

Can the same person be both wrong and right for you at the same time?

Saturday, February 7
7:30 P.M.

Amber showed up for work today half an hour late. Her face looked like a watercolor left out in the rain; mascara ran in long tracks down her cheeks, mixing with a thick putty of concealer.

"What's wrong?" I asked, grabbing her hands. "What happened? Something with Mr. Sands?"

She stared at her feet and shook her head, her long hair shielding her face. I craned my neck to see her better. Just as her bloodshot eyes met mine, I glimpsed what the concealer was intended to cover: a large, purplish bruise that spread out over her left cheekbone like an ink splotch.

"Jesus," I breathed. "Who did that?"

Her hand flew instinctively to the bruise, covering it with her fingers. "Shit. You can totally see it?"

"Yeah—I mean, it's huge. Who the hell—?"

But I heard a car drive up to the window then, and as she hunched over in the shadows, her body angled toward the wall, I went to take the order and get whoever it was out of there quickly so I could return to her.

Amazingly, it was Ben. Seven a.m. on a Saturday—the gray dawn still lingered—and there he was in a stocking cap, looking sleepy but adorable.

"Hey. What's up?" he said.

"Um, nothing. What are you doing here so early?"

He shrugged. "Couldn't sleep. Wanted to see you."

Oh, melt, melt, melt. Then I remembered that I had an emergency on my hands and shouldn't be swooning over my knight-in-white-stocking-cap. "That's sweet. Something's up with Amber, though. I can't really talk."

His face fell. "Are we back to this?"

"What? No—what do you—?"

"I get it. You two see each other constantly, but I try to steal five minutes and I'm out of luck."

"Ben!" What was happening? Was he jealous of Amber? Couldn't he see I had a serious situation to deal with? "Don't be ridiculous."

He shook his head and said in a husky, exhausted voice, "I just wanted to see you, but— Never mind, it was stupid."

"No, it's not stupid!" Behind me, I heard a muffled whimper escape from Amber. The five million things I wanted to say to Ben flooded my brain all at once, a massive Greek chorus gone berserk. What I finally choked out was, "Do you want some coffee?"

His sad smile broke my heart. "No, thanks. I hear it's not good for insomnia. Later, Sloane."

Just like that, he drove away! I whispered a string of curses and turned my attention back to Amber.

"You didn't tell him, did you?" she asked.

This seemed like a weird question, since Triple Shot Betty's is so small she must have heard our whole conversation, but I assured her I hadn't told him anyway.

"You can't say anything to anyone," she pleaded. "Not even your mom. Promise?"

"Okay, fine. But Amber—look at me—you've got to at least tell me what happened."

She shrugged, suddenly more composed, and pulled a compact from her purse. "It's not a big deal. This guy Danny just moved in."

"Is he your mom's boyfriend?"

"I guess you can call him that." She dampened a tissue at the sink and started cleaning her face with quick, efficient fingers. "Anyway, he got drunk last night, started playing 'Stairway to Heaven.' I told him if I heard that song one more time I'd slit my wrists. So he hit me."

"What did your mom do?"

"She yelled at him."

"Did she kick him out?"

"No. He hit her too. And then, you know, he begged forgiveness, blah, blah, blah." As she reapplied the concealer, her face took on a callousness that stirred in me a weird mixture of admiration and pity. She caught me staring and said in an irritated tone, "Don't look at me like that."

"I'm sorry, I just—"

"You just what?" she snapped.

"You shouldn't have to put up with that."

"Uh-huh. Okay. Well, thanks for that movie-of-the-week advice, but last time I checked, I don't really have any choice. Don't know if you've ever lived in a foster home, but believe me, it's not cool. *Comprende?*"

"So move in with us," I blurted out.

Her eyes left the mirror and found mine. For a second, the tough-girl façade slipped away and she said in a tiny, childlike voice, "Really?"

"Yeah."

"Do you think your mom would let—"

"Why not?"

She looked hopeful, but then a shadow passed over her face. "I don't want to drag you guys into this. My mom will freak out—it'll get totally messy."

"Amber," I said, my voice somber, "he hit you."

That was all it took. She broke down and cried like a little girl, her carefully applied makeup once again rendered a gooey mess. Wouldn't you know it—a string of cars queued up right then. I leaned over and whispered into her ear, "Walk to my house. The key's under the doormat in back. If Mom's gone, just let yourself in and chill. I'll be there as soon as I can."

She nodded, mopped at her face, and left.

As I served up cappuccinos, mochas, and lattes the rest of the morning, I asked myself the most dangerous of questions: How could things possibly get any more complicated?

Sunday, February 8
4:00 P.M.

Day one of cohabitation with Amber, and already I'm starting to wonder why this seemed like such a hot idea. I mean
yes, we had to get her away from the beastly step-boyfriend,
but man, when a household of two suddenly explodes to a
household of four, things get messy fast. No, Mungo hasn't
moved in officially, but he's here often enough to stake out a
shelf in the bathroom, and yesterday I spotted Mom folding
a load of his laundry. He's been doing most of the cooking
too, which is an improvement over Mom's inept efforts in the
kitchen. It just feels like things are changing so quickly. Our
once private, intimate little world has gotten all crowded and
complicated overnight.

Sharing a room with Amber makes one thing immediately
clear: The girl has clutter issues. Plus, her bathroom etiquette
leaves something to be desired; she's taken two showers here,
and already my shampoo has been depleted by half. Does
anyone have that much hair? But I tell myself these are the
small sacrifices we're forced to make in the name of sisterly
love.

Amber's mom showed up last night reeking of beer, bark-
ing orders at Amber and calling her names. Mom pulled her
into the kitchen, made a pot of coffee, and they talked for
over two hours. Amber and I hung back, waiting for an explosive Battle of the Matriarchs, but apparently they conversed
without violence. All Mom would say when we quizzed her

afterward was, "Your mother loves you, Amber. We agreed that you should stay here until she works some stuff out."

Uh, *yeah*. Step one: restraining order against sack-of-shit-who-beats-you.

But, you know, I'm trying not to be judgmental.

10:20 P.M.

Grabbed a quick taco with Ben downtown tonight, then skated the neighborhood for almost an hour. I practiced my ollies, but they're pretty rusty. I haven't really been skating as much since Ben and I started dating. What's up with that? I really need to get back out there and practice more, or I'll lose all my chops.

When I came back I found Amber on the floor of my— our!—room, bent over her sketchbook, scowling at something intently.

"What are you drawing?" I asked. "More tattoo designs?"

"Actually, I'm kind of working on a graphic novel."

"Wow, seriously?"

Amber tucked her chin shyly, flipping through her sketchbook. "It's just a rough draft . . ."

"Can I see?" I asked, sitting down beside her.

"Promise you won't laugh?"

Oh, gee, Amber, thanks for your faith in my sensitivity! "Of course I won't laugh."

"Okay, then." She flipped the pages of the sketchbook back until she'd reached the beginning. Then she handed it over, chewing on her bottom lip.

On the first page was a girl with long brown braids leaning

out the window of a drive-through espresso stand. I squinted
at the picture. It was definitely me—I'd recognize that Uniboob anywhere—except the caption read: "Georgia surveys
the parking lot as another hot summer day creeps by at Triple
Shot Betty."

In the next frame, two girls drove up in a shiny red Jeep;
they looked just like Bronwyn and Hero, except they were
named Bridget and Hannah. Soon Amber appeared—she'd
given herself the alias Amanda—and a catfight erupted between her and Hannah. I turned the pages, fascinated. Our
whole summer was there, captured in inky, dark contours,
shaded with colored pencils, our words floating in bubbles
over our heads. It was like finding a parallel universe peopled
with alternate versions of everything you recognize. She'd
named Sonoma Vinoville, and her character, Amanda, was a
tough Hell's Angel Princess who'd moved there from a town
called Wal-Mart City. The story line chronicled her adventures among the wealthy, sophisticated residents of Vinoville,
including her disastrous affair with a sinister senior named
James Johnson.

"This is fantastic!" I gushed. "I can't believe how well you
captured everything."

Amber shrugged. "It's really just doodles right now."

"You call this doodling? It's incredible." I got to the part
in the story where Ben drove up to the espresso stand in his
old Volvo, and I felt a lump in my throat, remembering how
happy I was when we first got together—before everything
became so messy. "It's amazing."

Amber rested her chin on her knees and peered at me cautiously. "You really like it?"

"I do! You're so talented."

She looked unconvinced. Her hand inched over and pulled the sketchbook back, like a child retrieving a favorite doll. "I showed it to Jeremy at work the other day. He reads a lot of comic books and graphic novels. He liked it."

"How could he not?"

"I wonder . . ." She trailed off.

"What?"

"I just wonder what Rex would say. You think he'd like it?"

Grrr. Why does Mr. Sands get to dictate what's cool in Amber's world? She used to be so outspoken, so sure of herself—or at least able to fake it when true confidence failed her. Ever since she started crushing on Mr. Sands, she's become a much mousier, less in-your-face version of herself. Is that what happens when people fall in love? Do they stop being themselves and start trying to be what someone else wants? Or is that just what happens when you fall for the *wrong* person?

"Who cares if he likes it or not?" My comment came out a lot snippier than I'd intended.

Her eyes went wide. "I do. Is that so wrong?"

I sighed. "It's not wrong, but don't you think doing what you love is more important than pleasing him? I mean, you're really good at this. You could maybe even do it as a job someday."

She shot me a skeptical look. "You think?"

"I do. And what does Mr. Sands know about graphic novels? Why should his opinion matter that much?"

"Oh, yeah," Amber scoffed. "What does he know? He's only got a PhD in literature."

I put a hand on hers. "I'm just saying, you shouldn't let him have so much power over you."

She pulled her hand back as if I'd stung her. "Thanks for the advice."

"Don't be mad."

"Look," she said tartly, "you never understood my feelings for him, so maybe we should just avoid talking about it."

"Fine." *Ouch.*

"Fine." She stuffed her sketchbook into her bag.

Monday, February 9
3:45 P.M.

After school, I skated up here to Geevana Ridge in search of sanity. There's a big white dragon of fog peeking its head over the western hills, getting ready to slither down into the valley, where it will spread its wings over everything. It smells good here today, like oak and eucalyptus. I just needed to get away from everything and everyone so I can think for a minute.

I really love this little meadow. I've been coming here since I was eleven, and it always makes me feel better. Back then I named the three oaks Gloria, Maxwell, and Albert; the rock at the end of the trail is called Hudson, and the iris that blooms every spring bears the highly inventive moniker Iris. I used to talk to them like they were friends. I was a preteen pagan, I guess.

Right now, I just need to sit on Albert's low, mossy trunk and not talk to anyone. It seems like everything in my life is making a concerted effort to be complicated lately. Why can't love ever be simple? Mom's all into Mungo, but who's to say they won't get sick of each other the way she and Dad did? Amber's obsessed with Mr. Sands, but she doesn't get that trying to please him makes her so much less interesting than she used to be. I thought things were back on track with Ben after our rainy Tuesday makeup session, but now this whole Valentine's dance after-party thing is freaking me out.

Nothing is simple anymore. It makes me want to go back to the olden days, when I could come up here with a bag of gummy worms and talk to the trees for hours. I guess I can't go back, though.

I just wonder if I'm really moving forward.

Tuesday, February 10
1:45 P.M.

Help! My persistent denial and procrastination have created a full-blown wardrobe crisis. The Valentine's dance is in four days, and I've got *nothing* to wear. As much as I hate, hate, *hate* the hysteria most girls succumb to before every dance, this time I'm forced to acknowledge a bitter truth: Refusing to plan ahead doesn't negate dance fever, it only postpones it.

I'm just not a frilly girl. Lace and taffeta make me feel like a drag queen.

In fifth period now, pulling the old diary-inside-the-history-book trick. Ben's right behind me. It's so hard to concentrate on the Vietnam War when I can almost feel his breath tickling the back of my neck. Do I really feel that, or is it the air vents?

Ms. Boyle keeps waving her arms around as she talks about Mai Lai. She's wearing a sleeveless Jimi Hendrix T-shirt, which shows off her tufts of armpit hair quite nicely. Ever since seeing her on a date with Mr. Sands, I can't look at her without wondering if she's kissed him. Amber's right. She really doesn't have any lips. How does one kiss a lipless person?

I wonder how far Ben expects me to go on Saturday? Presumably we'll have a bedroom all to ourselves. Do I really want to lose my virginity, then wake up to Sophie De Luca sneering at me over coffee? *Trés* romantic.

How am I going to break it to Mom that I'm not coming home?

I wonder if Ms. Boyle *wants* us to see her armpit hair in that shirt?

So many mysteries . . .

9:10 P.M.

Sixth period today got canceled for Battle of the Bands, a ritual that's theoretically entertaining but historically lackluster. The freshmen threw together a lame assortment of marching band plebeians, our own class displayed bad taste with a deeply ironic eighties cover band, and the seniors went so reggae you could almost smell the ganja billowing out of their instruments. The only showing worth talking about came from the sophomores. They got everyone's attention with a performance blending punk-ass courage with unapologetic romanticism—a winning combination, even with the Cynical Youth of Today.

Amber, Ben, PJ, and I sat there on the bleachers, trying to get into the spirit of things but failing miserably. Amber was wearing her Wonder Woman wig, which she kept scratching at in restless agitation. The gym always gets as humid as a South American jungle during rallies—all that pent-up adolescent angst—so Amber had to be dying in her rug.

"God, I just want to take this stupid thing off," Amber grumbled.

PJ looked at her. "Why are you wearing it, anyway? No offense, girl, but it looks a little like roadkill."

She jutted her chin out. "I'm feeling brunette! You got a problem with that?"

"Who am I to argue with that logic?" He leaned forward, elbows on his knees, shaking his head.

Ben laughed. "Is this some kind of sociology experiment?"

"Socio-what?" Amber asked.

"You know, like to see if you can start a fad, no matter how misguided and weird it is."

"Ben, are you calling me misguided and weird?"

PJ jumped to his friend's defense. "You're the one who said you wanted to take it off!"

Amber and I both scanned the crowded gym for Mr. Sands. When we didn't see him, we exchanged a look, and then she yanked the wig off impulsively, shaking out her own red hair and fluffing it with her fingers.

"Thank God," she said, "free at last!"

PJ smirked. "Did the brunette feeling pass?"

I laughed, and Amber slapped his arm, smiling. It made me strangely happy to see her unencumbered by her usual disguise. I mean, yeah, her elaborately constructed relationship

with Mr. Sands has a certain appeal; shrouded in secrecy,
built on deception, she never lacks for danger or intrigue.
All the same, I continue to think Amber would be happier
with someone less demanding. I'm no expert in the field, but
I know when I'm with Ben and I'm not worried about how
my hair looks or how my breath smells, I feel light and free
as a tuft of dandelion fur drifting on the wind. I hardly think
Amber gets that with Mr. Sands.

My attention snapped back to the festivities when I heard
Mr. Hardbaugh announce, "Next up we've got Nick Faller,
Suki Howell, Mark Woolman, and Jeremy Riggs doing a song
called 'Amber, Say Yes for Once.'"

Amber and I bit our lips at each other, and Ben shot us
a sideways glance but offered no comment. Behind our il-
lustrious principal seven or eight sophomores scurried about
madly on the makeshift stage, plugging in electrical chords
and flipping switches. A pimple-faced kid wearing John
Lennon glasses pushed a button and the contraption beneath
him started gushing fog, which swirled around the stage in
slow motion. Then the tech crew fell back and the girl behind
the drum kit said, "One, two, three" before she, the rhythm
guitar guy, and the bass player started up an insanely catchy
rhythm that had the whole room nodding their heads in time
within seconds.

The only person missing from the ensemble was Jeremy.
I looked around, afraid maybe he'd lost his nerve. I pictured
him crouched over a toilet in the boys' bathroom this very
minute, his face even whiter than usual.

And then I saw him.

I've been thinking about this for hours and I still don't

know how he did it. He just materialized there in the bleachers, mike in hand, black hair draped over one eye with rock star insouciance. A spotlight searched the gym, fell on him, and then the room went black except for the pool of silver light illuminating his skinny form. The gym exploded with shouts and applause. When the cheering had died down a little, Jeremy focused his piercing blue eyes on Amber and started to sing.

"She wears wigs like a secret agent,
I wonder who she's spying on.
Every day she's a different girl,
Identities she's trying on.
Her eyes are always full of secrets,
Green and moody as the sea,
I want to dive into that ocean,
But she never looks at me . . ."

Amber sat there with an expression of equal parts wonder and mortification. As if proving his lyrics true, she didn't dare look directly at Jeremy; instead her gaze moved from her shoes to me to the room at large, alighting only for seconds before flitting off in another direction like a skittish bird. By the time his posse on the stage kicked into high gear for the chorus, her face had gone so beet-red it practically glowed in the dark.

"Amber, say yes for once,
I know it's just a stupid dance,
But come on, say yes for once,
All I'm asking for is just one chance."

After the chorus, the spotlight went out abruptly, and Jeremy disappeared into a sea of black. Then a set of blue lights blazed to life on stage, and Jeremy came running up onto it, seized a black guitar, tossed the strap over his shoulder and plunged into an intricate solo that made the little hairs on the back of my neck stand up.

The entire auditorium went ballistic.

Jeremy Riggs: scrawny emo-kid, or rock legend?

Well, he got Amber to say yes for once, so I'm forced to assume he's a genius.

Wednesday, February 11
3:45 P.M.

Ben just texted me: *RU sure abt staying @ SDL's Sat nite?*

Grrrr. This whole Valentine's dance is turning into an extra-large pain in the butt with a side of humiliation. Not only do I have absolutely nothing to wear (thank you, Sophie De Luca, for making me hyper-aware of my dismal fashion sense) but I also have no idea what to do about this staying-over thing. And why does Ben have to keep bringing it up? Is he so determined to pop my cherry (to use the parlance of our times—disgusting!) that he just has to know right now whether or not I can accommodate? What, is Sophie waiting in the wings, eager to take my place in case I say no?

What's the big deal, anyway? I mean, jeez, I'm sixteen; I can do what I want! Sure, Mom will call the cops and ground me until I'm forty, but I can still make my own decisions.

Me: *Don't worry. I've got it under control.*

Ben: *She actually said yes?*

Me: *I told U, I don't have 2 ask!*

Ben: *Geena . . .*

Me: *The real problem is I have nothing 2 wear.*

Ben: *Sophie's going shopping in Corte Madera tmw after school. Maybe you should go with her.*

Oh my God! Is this boy utterly clueless? Doesn't he realize I'd rather ingest ground glass than go shopping with Sophie De Luca?

Me: *Gotta go. Talk later.*

Ben: *Okay. Just wanted U to know I'm thinking about U.*

Yeah, buddy, I get that. Sitting around thinking up ways to MAKE ME MISERABLE!!!

Thursday, February 12

8:45 P.M.

Amber and I went shopping in Santa Rosa after school today. I was in a foul mood, to tell you the truth. The last thing I wanted to do was cram my winter-bloated, blindingly white flesh into one tacky gown after another.

"So, we're all going to stay at the coast Saturday night?" Amber asked as she flipped through a rack of sale dresses. "Ben told me that's the plan."

So far my approach to the whole De Luca Sleepover Disaster has been consistent, if nothing else. I've been in total denial about it. If I continue to pretend it's not happening, it's not happening, right?

"I guess," I said vaguely.

Amber held up a white satin strapless dress for inspection. "Your mom's cool with it?"

Why am I stuck with the only mom on the planet who has a problem with this? Or rather, would have a problem with it, were anyone to mention it. "Yes. No. I don't know. Can we not talk about this?"

Amber gave me a funny look. She put the white satin back on the rack and pulled out a huge red taffeta monstrosity. "Do you even want to go?"

"Not really. But Ben wants to, I think. Is this cute?" I held up a bright yellow silk dress just to change the subject.

"Hideous. So what if Ben wants to go? Don't you have any say in it?"

I sighed. Clearly, Amber wasn't taking any hints. "I had to say yes."

"What do you mean?"

"Sophie asked us if we wanted to go and I knew Mom would have a cow, but what could I say? 'No, my mommy won't let me'?"

"So you lied."

"I'm just tired of Sophie always coming off as the mature one."

Amber shook her head. "Ben knows your mom. You should just tell him you can't go."

"It's kind of late now." Still hoping to nip this conversation in the bud, I stepped over to a bunch of mannequins sporting red and white dresses. One of them wore a huge, sparkly, heart-shaped hat on her molded plaster head. I picked up the hat and tried it on.

"What do you think? Is it me?" I posed for Amber.

She giggled. Then she saw something a little distance away and froze mid-giggle. "Oh, God! It's him."

"Who?"

"Rex! He's right over there."

I turned to follow her gaze and sure enough there he was, gliding slowly downward on the escalator, looking even more gorgeous than usual. Instinctively, I ducked behind a big rack of long dresses, hoping to avoid a conversation. I hadn't done my Camus essay yet, and I felt guilty about shopping instead of working on it.

"What are you doing?" Amber demanded, seeing me cowering behind the coats.

"Hiding."

"But why?"

"I don't want to see him!"

"*You* don't want to see him? Look at my outfit! Why did I wear this stupid shirt?"

"Hey, Amber," I heard Mr. Sands call out.

Amber turned away from me and waved reluctantly. "Hi, Rex. What are you doing here?"

I crouched down, hardly daring to breathe. From my vantage point I could see Amber standing there awkwardly, her hand on one hip.

"Oh, I just came to check out this bookstore I heard about. Thought I'd swing by and pick up some T-shirts while I'm here. Who were you talking to?"

"Talking to?"

"Yeah, when I came over, I thought you were talking to someone."

"Oh," Amber said, smiling stiffly. "I was on the phone."

He seemed to accept this. Very carefully, I peeked out from between two dresses, moving them just enough to see him grinning at her. I still had the ridiculous Valentine's hat on my head and had to stay crouched down in the tiny space between the dresses and the wall.

"Hey, I've been meaning to ask you, are you ever going to post another blog, or do I have to just keep reading that same one over and over?"

"Sure," she said. "I've just been busy."

"I love that part about Heathcliff being—what did you call him?"

"Oh . . . um . . . yeah, what did I . . . ?"

"The original sexy bad boy," I whispered frantically.

Amber echoed the line word for word, and we were rewarded with a wry, knowing chuckle from Mr. Sands. Ooh, it gave me goose bumps!

"You, uh, here all alone?" He stepped a little closer and lowered his voice slightly.

"No, I'm with a friend—but she's trying stuff on."

"I won't keep bugging you, then." He didn't move, though.

Amber grinned sweetly. "Okay then . . ."

"Okay."

"Nice seeing you."

"I'll call you," he promised, finally moving toward the exit.

She raised one hand and wiggled her fingers. "Okay. Bye!"

When he'd finally disappeared, we collapsed in a fit of giggles. So much for my efforts to dismantle our hopelessly warped love triangle.

We hunted for at least three hours before finally unearthing dresses we could live with at prices that wouldn't enrage our mothers. I tried to concentrate on the task at hand, but the whole time I kept hearing Mr. Sands's sweet, gravelly voice uttering those three syllables: "I'll call you."

Is it delusional to imagine the promise was also sort of meant for me?

Friday, February 13
9:50 P.M.

I sat at the kitchen table this afternoon, working on a Valentine for Ben. Amber has turned my room into one big walk-in floor-drobe, which makes it difficult to think in there. Normally, I keep things pretty tidy, but when you're sharing a room with a redheaded hurricane, it's pretty hard to maintain order.

Mom walked in all dressed up. She and Mungo were going to the city for dinner and a play. She smelled of lavender and was wearing a pretty pale green dress with sheer stockings and green suede pumps.

"What are you working on?" She poured herself a glass of wine and sat down across from me, killing time as she waited for Mungo.

I had a stack of magazines and old calendars, a glue stick, a pair of scissors, several sheets of construction paper, and a vial of gold glitter spread out before me on the table. So far, though, I hadn't done much with any of it. Between worrying about tomorrow night and feeling guilty about posting another blog last night to Amber's page for Mr. Sands, I couldn't seem to get inspired.

"I'm trying to make a valentine for Ben."

"How's it going?" She took another sip of her merlot, glancing at the empty page before me.

"*Comme ci comme ca.*"

I knew I should just bite the bullet and ask Mom if I could stay at the coast tomorrow night. I rehearsed openers in my head: *Mom, I know you're not going to like this, but . . .* No, that would set off alarms immediately. *Hey, you know how I've been so understanding about you and Mungo practically living together?* Thinly veiled guilt-inducer—she'd see right through it. *Mom, I'm sixteen and should be allowed to go off and have drunken, sloppy sex at someone's beach house if I feel like it.*

"What's the matter, pumpkin? You look so worried."

Okay, I told myself, it's now or never. I took a deep breath and opened my mouth, but what came out was, "Are you getting Mungo something for Valentine's Day?"

She grinned. "Yeah. You want to see?"

I nodded. She darted back to her room and came out with a gift bag covered with tiny cupids. "I got him these . . ." She pulled out a pair of boxer shorts in a bright red heart pattern. "Cute, right? And this ..." Out came a silky black T-shirt. Then she started blushing and clutched the bag a little tighter. "That's all."

"Wait a second," I said. "There's still something in there."

"Nope. That's it." She's such a bad liar. Guess I know where I get my sucky-with-secrets gene.

I grabbed at the bag and she protested. "Geena, it's noth—"

I fished the last item from the bag and pulled it free of the tissue paper. It was a hardcover copy of *The Kama Sutra.*

Auugh! Why had I insisted on looking? I so did not want to think about my mother and Mungo studying up on a variety of Hindi scripture—recommended sexual positions.

"Nice." I employed a tone that I hoped communicated just how done I was with the conversation.

"Well, you insisted."

I couldn't argue with that.

"Is everything okay?" She stuffed the gifts back into the bag, her brow furrowed. "You seem preoccupied or something."

Once again, I tried to make myself ask her about staying at Sophie's, but I just couldn't force my mouth to form the words. "I'm fine. I want to make Ben a cool card, only I'm not very artistic. It's frustrating." This was true, though not the whole picture, obviously.

"Maybe you should concentrate on the message." She reached over and gently tugged one of my braids. "Tell him something from your heart. You can't go wrong with that."

Just then the doorbell rang, and her expression switched instantly from wise and maternal to hyper as a twelve-year-old on too much sugar. She grabbed her clutch. "There he is. We'll be home sort of late. There are burritos and a salad in the fridge for you and Amber."

"Okay. Have fun."

"We will. Be good!" And then she was gone.

I stared at the blank pieces of construction paper before me. Maybe she was right. I should focus on the message first, and worry about making it look good later. When Amber got home from her shift at Floating World she could help me with the artwork, probably.

Dear Ben,

This is the first valentine I've given someone since elementary school. I hope it turns out all right. There are so many things I want to tell you, but I'm afraid that even if I memorize every single word on the SAT vocabulary list I still won't find the right ones to express myself here.

As you know, I'm not really a girlfriend kind of girl—or at least, I haven't been until now. I'm afraid I've been sort of bad at it, seeing as I'm a beginner. I want you to know that if I seem weird or unaffectionate or uptight sometimes, it isn't because of you. I'm just so used to being independent and taking care of myself—not worrying about anyone else—that I don't really know how to let someone in. Does that make sense?

Being with you, there's so much to navigate: excitement and jealousy and insecurity, lust and fear and unexpected bursts of joy. It's like finding myself at the top of a fifteen-foot vertical ramp, staring straight down into the bowl, wondering how I'm going to get down. I mean, there's really no way to do it except just to <u>do it</u>, right? All the same, you can't blame me for being a little scared.

Anyway, I hope this explains some of my more awkward moments in the past few months and that you'll forgive me if I'm weird in the future. Really, I can't imagine figuring this stuff out

*with anyone except you. It's not always easy being
a girlfriend, but you make it totally worth it.*

      Love,

        Geena (aka Valedictorian to be)

"Hey, G."

I looked up and saw Amber in the doorway. I'd been so engrossed in my letter I hadn't even heard her come in. "Hi. Did you just get here?"

"Yeah. I'm starving."

I realized suddenly that my stomach was grumbling. "Me too. Mom said there are burritos and salad in the fridge."

She yanked the refrigerator door open and started taking things out. "What are you doing?"

"Writing a valentine for Ben. Can you help me make it look cool?"

"Yeah. That'll be fun." She unwrapped a burrito, set it on a plate, and put it in the microwave. "You ask your mom about staying at Sophie's yet?"

I groaned. "No. She'll never go for it anyway, so there's really no point."

"Jeremy can't go either—not that I wanted to spend the night out there with him. Don't want him getting ideas. They can just drop us off here before they head out, right?"

"Oh, so Ben's going to stay at Sophie's without me?" I pulled a face. "I don't *think* so."

She leaned against the counter and looked at me. "You know, G, you've got to get over this Sophie weirdness. I really don't think Ben would ever go for her."

"They messed around."

"Before he ever got together with you," she reminded me. "That doesn't count."

"Hmm," I said, not convinced.

"Seriously." She picked a piece of celery out of the salad and popped it into her mouth. "You should just trust him."

I put my burrito into the microwave, set the time, and watched it slowly rotate. "Easier said than done."

Saturday, February 14
2:30 P.M.

This morning at work, our boss showed up for the first time in a while. He's been in Maui for two weeks, sunning himself and drinking mai-tais, or whatever people do in Maui. It must have been something good, because when he drove up in his racer green MINI Cooper he looked so tan and relaxed I barely recognized him.

"Hey, Lane!" I called when he drove up to the window. "Long time no see. You look fabulous."

"You're too kind." He tilted his Wayfarers down and studied me over the rims. "You Bettys staying out of trouble? Did Joe keep everything stocked? Are you maintaining sanitary conditions in there?"

"Pretty sanitary. We shooed most of the rats out and made friends with the cockroaches."

"Hardee-har-har. You know what to do, Geena. Work your fairy magic on a double cappuccino, will you?" He handed me his fancy to-go mug.

"Aye, aye, captain!"

Lane likes us to look busy, no matter how slow things get, so Amber got up off her stool and started wiping down everything in sight. She even tried to run her rag over me, but I slapped her away.

"Be good, girls," Lane called, "or you won't get your treats!"

When I handed back his to-go mug, Lane tucked it into his cup holder, then handed over two small containers of chocolate-covered macadamia nuts, each with a little heart attached, our names printed out on them in Lane's curly cursive.

"Oh," Amber said, seizing hers. "Thank you!"

"Yeah, thanks, Lane."

"Happy Valentine's Day." Another car drove up behind him and he shifted gears. "I think it's a perfectly hideous holiday, but if anyone should enjoy it, it's my two favorite Bettys. Tah-tah!"

6:40 P.M.

Oh. My. God.

Mother Nature gave me perfectly workable eyebrows. I have worn these eyebrows for the past sixteen years and they've never let me down. Now, though, in the clutches of Sophie De Luca fever, I've defiled them! Oh, good Lord, what possessed me?!

It started with a little innocent grooming. Amber and I were getting ready for the dance, experimenting with different hairstyles and makeup effects. Mom and Mungo went hiking in Saint Helena, so we had the whole house to ourselves. After work, we turned the place into Spa Geember. It was fun, to tell you the truth. We cranked up the music as loud as it would go and gave each other oatmeal facials with a recipe we got online. We even did the full-on mani-pedi routine, helping each other choose the perfect shade of polish to go with our dresses. We don't really indulge in such hyper-girlie activities that often, so it was fun going all out.

The whole time, though, in the back of my mind, one thought haunted me: I still haven't asked Mom about staying out at the coast tonight. What's the point? Obviously, she'll say no. Once that happens, I'll either have to admit to Ben et al that I completely lied and come home by my curfew like a preteen brat, or I'll have to defy her commands openly and face house arrest until I'm forty. Excellent choices. Thank you, Sophie De Luca, for wedging me between this rock and proverbial hard place.

Oh, and if that isn't bad enough, now we're actually going to the dance *with* Sophie and PJ! *Quelle horreur.* I'm sure my red jersey wrap dress is going to look so infantile next to whatever she wears. Let's not sugarcoat it; Sophie is Satan, plain and simple.

Underneath, though, I'm wearing the camisole and underwear Ben gave me for Christmas. Not that he'll see them, necessarily. Still, they're under there, secret reminders that—back in December, anyway—he cared enough to give me custom-made lingerie.

But I digress. Ben and the others will pick us up in ten minutes, so I'd better get this down. My eyebrows! My God, my eyebrows!

All I wanted to do was shape them a little, like Sophie's. I mean come on, I've got a 4.0 GPA, how hard could it be? While Amber was blow-drying her hair I nabbed Mom's tweezers and got to work.

"Ow!" The first couple hairs were brutal. I'd never tweezed anything in my life, so I wasn't exactly prepared.

Amber turned the blow-dryer off. "What's wrong?"

"Nothing. Just tweezing." I could feel a little tingle in the tip of my nose and tears were stinging my eyes, but I went on systematically ripping the hairs out anyway. I'd never noticed it before, but I've actually got quite bushy brows. As I thinned them out, I started to feel more confident. *See?* I thought. *Being beautiful isn't rocket science. All you have to do is make an effort.*

Five minutes later, Amber turned off the blow-dryer, caught sight of my reflection in the mirror, and gasped. "G! What are you doing?"

"What does it look like I'm—"

"They're not symmetrical! Your left eyebrow is higher than the right."

I studied myself in the mirror. She wasn't lying. My face looked as lopsided as a Picasso. I felt panic starting to blossom inside my rib cage. "Shit."

"Here, let me try." She grabbed the tweezers from my hand and started plucking. Her face scrunched up in concentration and her tongue stuck out just a tiny bit as she worked. Her body was between me and the mirror, so I just closed my eyes and prayed she could fix them.

"There," she said. "That's better."

I looked at her, hope dawning. "Really?"

She took half a step back and surveyed her work. At first she looked pleased, but then, as she took in my whole face, her expression became gradually more disturbed. She still blocked my view of the mirror. I tried to breathe normally and not give in to the dread that threatened to overwhelm me.

"What's wrong?" I asked in a tiny voice.

"Now they match, at least."

"What do you mean, 'at least'?"

"They're definitely . . . not bushy."

The girl was grasping at straws now, obviously. I summoned all my courage and stepped around her so I could see for myself.

There, in the mirror, my face stared back at me. Only it wasn't my face, exactly. I mean, it was me, but my eyebrows were now so sparse, they looked like they'd been drawn on with a ballpoint pen that was running out of ink. Not only that, but they were way up on my forehead, so that I looked even more surprised than I actually was.

I couldn't help it. I screamed.

Damn! There's the door. More later.

Sunday, February 15
1:15 P.M.

When Ben picked us up, the first thing I saw was his happy, smiling face, his dark eyes shining in the porch light. Then I noticed Sophie, PJ, and Jeremy standing together in the shadows on the steps behind him. I made myself concentrate just on Ben for a second, though I was dying to check out Sophie's dress. He looked so cute. More than cute, really—gorgeous. He wore a suede coat, a crisp white shirt with a patterned tie, and pressed chinos. He smelled clean and soapy. Something in his smile seemed a bit wobbly and nervous, which made me feel a little better about the butterflies swooping through my belly.

"Hey," I said.

"Hey, yourself." His eyes scanned my body, but in a sweet way, not skeevy or anything. Then he noticed my eyebrows and he looked a little startled, but he covered it up well. "You look beautiful."

I shrugged one shoulder, wishing to God I'd never touched those stupid tweezers.

I was counting on Mom staying out with Mungo until late. I pointedly insisted they take their time in St. Helena, go get some dinner after their hike, and had calculated that there was no way our paths would cross before the dance. Ha! Just as I was calling to Amber that it was time to go (she was putting nail polish on a last-minute run in her stockings) what should appear in the driveway? You guessed it: Mungo's Volvo.

"Hi there," Mom called, scrambling out of the passenger's side while Mungo got out from behind the wheel. "I'm so glad we caught you. Let's take some pictures!"

"No time, Mom," I protested. "We'll be late for dinner."

Ben, ever-charming, smiled as my mother dashed inside for her camera. "We're okay," he said. "We've got fifteen minutes."

To my credit, I pasted on a brave face, realizing it was futile to protest. Five minutes of obligatory photos and we'd be out of there. "Okay. Come on in."

Sophie stepped out of the shadows then and I nearly shielded my eyes, she was so luminous. Her shimmery silver dress was festooned with sequins; it was a bit like the black one she'd worn at Christmas, only this one was even more flattering, if that was possible. Her endless legs looked longer than ever in strappy silver stilettos. I never would have had the guts to try an outfit like that; on her, though, it was pure magic.

"Hi, Sophie." I tried to unclench my jaw. "You look great."

She gave me the quickest, most dismissive once-over in the history of once-overs, not even bothering to hide her disdain when she saw my botched plucking job. "You too."

PJ nodded to me in greeting. He looked smooth in a dark leather jacket, a red silk shirt, and black slacks. "Hey, chica. What happened to your eyebrows?"

Instinctively, I covered them with one hand. "Long story."

"Sorry about that."

I could feel my cheeks going hot. Well, I'd better get used to it.

Behind PJ stood Jeremy, all nervous and cute as usual. He wore tight, straight-legged pants, a colorful, retro print shirt, and a blue blazer that matched the streak in his bangs.

Amber came busting out of my room. "Damn these stockings! I knew I shouldn't have gotten the drug store kind. Whatever, they'll have to do. Hi, you guys."

Everyone said hello. I saw Jeremy's eyes light up as he took in Amber in her funky yellow dress. She looked good. They were unmistakably perfect side by side—sort of offbeat and rebellious and not matching at all but somehow matched. I couldn't help thinking that Sophie and Ben looked like they belonged together more than Ben and me. She'd just stepped out of *Elle*, he was all *GQ*, and I looked sort of, well, Wicked Witchy. Who didn't belong in this picture?

"Okay, here we go, one couple at a time!" Mom came running into the living room with her camera.

Sophie and PJ posed first, then Amber and Jeremy, then Ben and me. Mom went on about how cute we all were, tactfully not mentioning the fact that I'd totally mutilated the eyebrows God gave me. She took what seemed like five thousand shots. We were halfway to the door when she called out, "Oh, wait, let's get a group shot!"

"Mother," I groaned. "Enough!"

"Please? Indulge your old mom, will you?"

I sighed and we all squeezed together in front of the fireplace, arranging our faces into careful smiles. That's when the bomb dropped.

"It's so nice of you to let Geena stay over at our place tonight," Sophie cooed, her eyes still fixed on the camera.

My stomach did like five back flips in a row. I couldn't breathe. I couldn't speak.

Slowly, Mom's face emerged from behind the lens. "I'm sorry, what was that?"

The room filled with the most deafening silence ever. I knew I should say something, but I had no idea what that something might be. It was like watching a car crash in slow motion.

Sophie brushed her hair back from her face. "I said I'm glad you're letting Geena stay over. With the rest of us. At our house on the coast?"

Mom's smile went twitchy. "The coast?"

"Uh . . ." Ben stepped in, glancing at me. "After the dance? We're all going out to Sophie's family's house in Bodega. That's okay, right?"

Shit!

"Oh my God." I slapped my forehead. "Mom, didn't I tell you that? I could have sworn I mentioned it."

No luck. Mom's face just got twitchier. "No. I'm quite sure you didn't."

Amber said, "Well, we better get going."

"Yeah, we probably should," Jeremy agreed.

I shot them a grateful look.

Mom addressed Ben in a grave, no-nonsense tone. "I don't think I'm prepared to let my sixteen-year-old daughter stay out all night. Amber, while you're living here you'll have the same curfew. Have them home by one?"

"Mom . . ." It was useless, though. Normally, she'd let me stay out later than that for a special occasion, but she was pissed about the subterfuge, I could tell. I didn't even bother to protest beyond that single syllable.

"Sure, Mrs. Sloane," he told her. "No problem."

As we made our way to Sophie's Mercedes, I knew I'd rather fling myself under the wheels of the next passing car than endure another second of my misery. Sophie whispered something to PJ before she allowed herself a catty little giggle. Ben wouldn't look at me. I just shuffled along, me and my ridiculous eyebrows, the girl who couldn't stay out past one, the biggest loser on the planet.

The night had barely begun, and already I wanted to die.

○ ● ● ○ ● ○

We drove to Cafe La Haye with Sophie's music blaring. That was just as well. I found myself missing the suntan oil and damp dog scent of Ben's rusty old Volvo. The Mercedes smelled like new leather overlain with all the gels, lotions, and deodorants we'd plied ourselves with, and the potent combination gave me a headache. I cracked the window slightly, feeling claustrophobic. A heaviness started to gather force inside me.

As we got out of the car and everyone started toward the restaurant, I touched Ben's arm. "Hey, don't be mad."

"Why should I be?"

Amber laughed at something Jeremy said. Sophie bent her head toward PJ and whispered something again. We let the four of them walk a little ways ahead of us.

"I meant to ask—I just wanted to find the right—" I started.

"You told me it was okay."

"I know. I didn't want to disappoint you, so I just . . ." My sentence trailed off lamely.

"Lied."

The flat, hard sound of his voice caught me off guard. "Well, not exactly."

"Yes, exactly."

I looked at him, and his face suddenly seemed foreign. A hard, opaque black replaced the luminous warmth his eyes usually radiated. A little muscle in his jaw pulsed. I suddenly felt small, exposed, and defenseless there in my pitiful made-in-China dress and painful patent-leather shoes. A breeze washed over us. I shivered. We stared at each other in silence.

"Whatever." He looked away. "It's no big deal."

For some reason my mood somersaulted right then from apologetic to pissed off. Maybe it was the tiny, sarcastic curve of his lips—I don't know—but a switch flipped inside me and all at once we went from couple-having-a-tiff to enemies.

"Fine," I sniffed, matching his terse, cold tone. "Let's go inside."

Dinner was torture. Amber and Jeremy got along great. They debated the merits of various high-profile tattoo artists and gossiped about Floating World. They discovered a mutual love of several obscure British punk bands, and they were off on that for at least an hour, quoting lyrics, trying to one-up each other with little-known trivia. Sophie flirted with Ben and PJ both, soaking up their attention, flashing me a tiny, triumphant smile every now and then when nobody else was looking. I sat like a carved statue and gazed at the ever-fascinating bread basket.

When our food came, I could barely pick at my pan-roasted chicken breast with goat cheese stuffing. I sliced into it with my knife very carefully, peeling back the flesh as if performing an autopsy. I moved it around on my plate, trying to make it look like I'd eaten some. I cut it into tiny pieces and concealed it inside my mashed potatoes.

I told myself that if Ben said something to me—anything— I'd apologize for real the second I could get him alone. If he said so much as "pass the salt" I'd take it as a sign. I'd admit everything in gory detail: my stupid, misguided crush on Mr. Sands, my fear that he's in love with Sophie and only stays with me out of pity, my babyish inability to ask Mom about staying at the coast. He didn't speak to me, though. He barely even looked at me. He concentrated entirely on PJ and Sophie. It was as if I'd become invisible somewhere between the car and Cafe La Haye. I sat there, a ghost of a girl, able to hear and see but unable to speak or be seen.

By the time we got to the dance I felt so depressed I could barely drag myself from the car. It was held at the Vintage House, this senior center that rents out its shadowy, cavernous main hall for dances and stuff. The sophomores had gone with this rather confusing futuristic Valentine's Day motif. Evidently the wild profusion of tinfoil hearts and black lights were supposed to convince us we'd been transported to some exotic futurescape. Couples posed before a cold silver and white backdrop, pointing plastic laser guns at the camera with manic smiles.

Amber and Jeremy headed straight for the dance floor, where black lights turned everyone's teeth into searing, glow-in-the-dark grins. Seizure-inducing strobes kicked into gear every few seconds, making me feel sort of sick. Sophie and PJ went to get Cokes from the bar. Ben and I leaned against the wall, draped in shadow. I wondered if he felt as bewildered and alone as I did.

"I guess you don't want to dance," was all he said.

"Not really, no."

"Me neither."

There we were: ranked top in our class, with combined test scores higher than the national debt, and our vocabularies had been reduced to these paltry syllables. Soon we'd be grunting and pounding our chests.

We sat down on a couple of folding chairs festooned with

limp streamers. As Amber and Jeremy got down to some vintage funk, I saw past the fog of my own wretchedness long enough to notice how perfect they were together. They had distinct styles—Jeremy was sort of understated-ironic, whereas Amber had an exuberant, disco-inferno flamboyancy—yet they complemented each other perfectly. Their bodies took on a mutual grace no one around them could match, as if the music held inside it a secret language only they understood.

"Happy Valentine's Day, Benedict!" Sophie came back with two Cokes in plastic cups and handed one to Ben. With a quick glance around, she pulled a silver flask from her purse and tipped a generous splash into Ben's drink.

"Whoa," Ben protested. "I thought you wanted me to drive."

"You still can," Sophie assured him. "I only gave you like half a shot."

PJ handed me a Coke too. He met my eye, the first person to really look at me all night, and I could see he felt sorry for me. "How you doing, Skater Girl?"

I almost burst into tears. His basic human kindness made me want to fall at his feet in a heap. Instead I bit my lip and said, "Okay. You?"

"Not bad."

Sophie turned to me, her huge white smile gleaming. "Geena, you don't mind if I borrow Benedict for a teensy-weensy dance, do you?"

"Why not?"

Ben shot me a quick look, though in the wonky, strobe-effect lighting I couldn't be sure of his expression. Then he followed Sophie out to the dance floor like an obedient dog. Just as they reached the thicket of bodies pumping and writhing to the heavy bass beat, the DJ did a slow cross fade from Fergie to the timeless sap of the Honeydrippers' "Sea of Love."

Watching Sophie eagerly fold herself into his arms, a dark sense of foreboding washed over me. I saw Ben hesitate slightly, then obligingly wrap his perfectly sculpted arms around her waist.

Suddenly I craved my skateboard intensely. I wanted to trade this stupid dress for my cut-off Dickies and a T-shirt. I needed to fly through the dark streets, the damp air streaming over me. I could almost feel my board vibrating under my Pumas, the instinctive tightening in my calves and quads as I crouched low on the descent, dancing with gravity, daring it to mess with me. I knew the rotting leaves and wet cement would mix together inside my head, and the steady, white-noise sound of my wheels would soothe this terrible churning in my gut.

"You sure you're okay, Geena?" PJ asked.

"I'm fine."

Out on the dance floor, Sophie did a twirl and then a dip, hamming it up, and I could see Ben smiling. Then she nestled even more snugly into his arms.

PJ chuckled. "Sophie's really something."

"She sure is," I said.

"Bummer about the coast."

I watched as Sophie nuzzled Ben's neck, and the sick feeling in my stomach intensified. "Yeah. Total bummer."

"You want to dance?" PJ asked.

I could feel tears stinging at my eyes. I needed to get out of there. "No, thanks. I'm going to get some air."

As soon as I stepped outside, I felt a little better. Sometime during our internment inside the Vintage House it had started to rain, and as I stood there under the fluorescent-lit overhang it came down in sheets. I still had my coat on; at the edge of the dance floor it made me feel bulky and awkward, but out here I was glad for it.

I reached into my inside pocket and pulled out Ben's valentine. Last night Amber helped me make the coolest collage, a mix of photographs we cut out and pictures she drew. It was all stuff Ben loved: cyclists racing in the Tour de France; Frankenstein's monster; the canals of Venice; a pale brown Chihuahua that looked just like his dog, Mr. Peabody. The whole time we were working on it, I kept imagining his face when he opened it, picturing the way his expression would soften as his eyes scanned the images. I could imagine so perfectly the way his lips would move ever so slightly as he read what I'd written inside. Now I couldn't picture any of that.

"Hey." I turned to see Amber at my elbow, her face a question mark. "You okay?"

I quickly stuffed Ben's card back into my pocket. "I guess."

"Why is Ben dancing with Sophie? What's up with you two? You're acting like you hate each other."

"We're having a really off night."

"Seriously!" Amber wiped her damp forehead with her arm. "Jesus, I'm sweating like a pig."

"You and Jeremy sure are hitting it off."

"Yeah, he's cool." She used a dismissive, no-big-deal tone

and immediately boomeranged the subject back to me. "What are you guys fighting about, anyway?"

"The whole beach house thing, I guess."

Her eyes widened. "Oh my God, that was awful. At your house? Your mom looked pissed."

"Yeah," was all I said.

"What's the big deal with Ben, though? So you can't go to the coast. Why should you guys fight over that?"

"I should have told him earlier, that's all."

"Hello! Didn't I say that?"

"Yes, you told me so; yes, I screwed up; yes, I suck." I put my hand on one hip. "Happy now?"

"Jeez, don't get mad at *me*."

"I'm not." I blew my hair out of my eyes in frustration. "But this whole thing is turning into a major nightmare."

Just then the door swung open and Ben came out. He caught the last part of my sentence and I saw the little muscle in his jaw throb again.

"Alrighty, then," Amber said, spinning toward the door. "I'm outta here."

When she'd gone, Ben and I stared out at the rain, not speaking. It was like we'd lost a common language. I thought of pulling out his valentine and handing it over, an olive branch, a white flag, but it felt all wrong. I wanted to give it to him not as an apology, but as an offering—something separate from this mess.

Ben stuffed his hands into his pockets. Still staring out at the rain, he said, "I just don't get why you lied to me."

"I don't know . . . It didn't seem that important." I knew this was weak, but it was all I could manage.

"It was important to me. I wanted tonight to be . . . really great."

"What, you, me, and Sophie?" I made a sound in my throat. I should have apologized, I knew that, but a dark anger welled up inside me, poisoning my words. "How romantic!"

"What do you have against her? She likes you."

"Ha!"

"Except you get so weird around her." He hazarded a glance at me now. "You're not yourself when she's in the room."

God! Was he being intentionally moronic? "She's totally after you! Can you seriously not see that?"

"Sloane, I told you a million times, we're just old friends."

"Friends with benefits?"

He massaged his forehead. "Just that one time in Tahoe. It was nothing. I swear to God, Geena, I don't even think about her like that."

I looked away. "If you say so."

"What about you and Doctor Hipster?" He turned on me abruptly, his tone harsh. "I see how you look at him in English. You think that doesn't bug me?"

"I— Wait a second—"

"And you tell Amber more than you ever tell me! It's like you two are the couple, not us."

"Amber's my best—"

"Friend," he finished. "I know. But the point is, you open up with her, and you don't with me. Maybe at first you did, but not lately. You treat me like an enemy."

My mind spun in circles. Was he right about me being

more open with Amber than I was with him? I couldn't even speak. I knew if I did I'd say something stupid or incriminating.

"Tonight was supposed to be . . . I don't know, not this," he said. "And now you can't even come to Bodega."

My temper flared again. "Okay, let me ask you this: Why does staying at Bodega matter so much? Has my virgin expiration date expired?"

He recoiled. "What? That's what you think?"

"Oh, come on, Ben! What else were we going to do out there? Study for the SATs?"

He sighed and ran a hand through his hair. "You know, maybe this isn't working."

My stomach dropped. I felt like I might throw up. When I thought I could speak without a quiver in my voice I said, "What do you mean?"

"I mean you don't seem that into it."

"Into what, exactly?"

"Into me." He glanced at me quickly, and I thought I saw tears shining in his eyes.

I pulled at a strand of hair and started chewing on it. A part of me wanted to fling myself into his arms and wail that he was wrong, that I'm totally into him, that the thought of breaking up makes my heart contract with terror and misery. The other part of me wondered if he was right. If I'm so into him, why do I lust after Mr. Sands? Why did I risk upsetting him with this stupid lie? Why *do* I open up more easily with Amber than I do with him? Either I'm not that into him, or I'm just really, really bad at being a girlfriend. Both possibilities led to the same dreary, dead-end conclusion: It wasn't working.

I took a deep breath. "Are you saying you want to break up?"

The silence stretched on for so long, I almost repeated the question, but finally he said, "Maybe that's the best thing. Before things get—you know—ugly."

I felt that tingly pressure in my head, a warning that I'd be crying any second. Once that happened I knew every last shred of my dignity would dissolve. I had to escape.

The door opened and Sophie leaned out, her sequins sparkling in the streetlight. "Ben-e-dict!" she sang in a tipsy voice.

"Give us a minute," Ben told her roughly.

"Oops! So sorry." She headed back inside, but I heard her say to someone in a confidential tone, "They're having a *talk*."

All my sadness turned into a flood of rage, suddenly. I felt it pulsing inside my veins, coursing through my system. "Well, I won't take up more of your time."

"Geena—" He reached for me, but I shrugged him off.

"Here." I pulled his card from my pocket and started to shred it. I tore it into smaller and smaller pieces, then tossed them at him like a fistful of confetti. "Happy Valentine's Day, *Benedict!*"

With that I ran out into the rain.

○ ⦁ ⦁ ○⦁ ○

Walking home, my dress got totally soaked and clung to my skin like a layer of Saran Wrap. Luckily, the dance was only about five blocks from my house. Halfway home, though, I got so sick of my cheap, uncomfortable girlie shoes that I kicked them off and left them in the gutter. I knew it was wasteful, but they were ruined anyway. It's not like I'd ever wear them again.

Only when I'd made it safely inside and stood panting in the dimly lit foyer did I allow myself to let loose. The strangled sob that escaped my lips was so wretched, I hardly knew it was coming from me.

Right away, Mom appeared in a lavender nightgown I'd never seen before. She hugged me tightly, and when the worst of my racking sobs had passed, she gripped my shoulders and pulled away so she could study me. "What happened, pumpkin?"

I looked at her. The expression she wore was solemn and knowing. I didn't trust myself to speak, so I just shook my head.

She took in my wet dress and muddy, bare feet. "Did somebody hurt you?"

I knew what she was asking. She didn't mean *Did Ben Bettaglia tear your heart out and stomp it into a bloody pulp?* She meant *Did someone give you date rape drugs and have his way with you?* I shook my head again.

She pulled me to her and stroked my hair. "Love is hard, isn't it?"

I just nodded.

"I know," she whispered into my part. "I know."

2:40 A.M.

I feel a little bit better now, but not much. I took a hot shower and told Mom the basics over a cup of hot chocolate. She dished out a lackluster scolding for the Bodega thing,

I could tell her heart wasn't in it, though. She'd have to be pretty hard-hearted to skewer me just for *thinking* about staying out all night. I hadn't actually done it, after all. Laughing until dawn, running through the moonlit dunes, drinking from a silver flask—those were things girls like Sophie De Luca did. Apparently, I'm the sort of girl who kicks her shoes into the gutter and drags her sorry ass home before midnight.

Amber came into my room about ten minutes after I'd turned out the light. I could hear her taking off her dress, mumbling curses at her ruined stockings, and then I knew she was putting on the big, threadbare Rocky Horror Picture Show T-shirt she always sleeps in.

"G?" She sat on my bed in the dark. "You awake?"

I thought about feigning sleep, but decided that was dumb. I rolled over to face her. "Yeah."

She turned on the bedside lamp. "You've been crying. Poor thing."

Her unexpected sympathy made me feel like sobbing again, but I swallowed the urge and forced a little smile. I'd already used up my patheticness quota for the day. "Did you have fun?"

"Yeah, I guess, but what happened to you? Ben told me you broke up."

I just nodded. Hearing it like that made it seem more official—more final. More horrible, if that was possible.

"He borrowed Sophie's car and went looking for you."

"He did?" I propped my head up with one hand.

She nodded. "He was really upset. Sophie tried to talk him into going out to the coast, but he got a ride home with one of the stofers instead. I don't think anyone went out there, in the end. PJ had to drive me, Sophie, and Jeremy home. She got a little wasted."

"Did she do anything stupid?" I asked hopefully.

"She almost tripped. No wonder, though—those stilettos were total stilts!" She peered at me carefully. "What happened? Why did you guys break up?"

I flopped back against my pillow. "I don't know. I guess we just don't communicate very well."

"Okay, that's way too vague. Spill."

"I'm serious," I told her. "There's no specific reason. We just bickered about the coast thing and Sophie, and he accused me of not being that into him."

"Who actually said, 'Let's break up'?"

"He did."

She shook her head. "I can't believe that. This is the guy who had me design a Geena Sloane logo so he could give you one-of-a-kind underwear! He's crazy about you."

"Not anymore." I felt myself wanting to cry again, so I covered it with a hard little laugh. "Maybe it was the eyebrows."

"I'm sorry, G." She squeezed my shoulder.

I changed the subject. "You and Jeremy were so cute together."

"Whatever." She rolled her eyes. "He's fun, but we're not like that."

"Did he kiss you?"

"No! Of course not. You know I'm all about Rex. I can't lead Jeremy on—that would be cruel."

"Yeah," I said, disappointed. "I guess."

⚬ ● ● ⚬ ● ⚬

She's passed out on the futon now and I'm finally getting sleepy. God, what a night. I've started to text Ben five or six times, but haven't actually managed to hit SEND on any of my pathetic attempts. Really, what am I going to say? Even if I knew what I wanted to tell him, I doubt I could express it in a text message.

Happy Valentine's Day to me.

4:45 P.M.

It's been raining for like twenty hours straight. Thank God. I don't think I could handle one of those sparkly, exhilarating, cloudless winter days that makes everyone want to fly a kite or climb the nearest mountain. No, instead Black Sunday dawned in a downpour.

Amber, Mom, and I rented five movies, all of them lightweight enough to vanish from my memory bank even as the final credits rolled—celluloid cotton candy. Normally, Mom prefers meandering BBC-type films with lots of eyebrow acting by less-than-attractive people. This morning, though, she took one look at my puffy, bloodshot eyes and immediately launched a campaign to cheer me up. She sent Mungo home with a kiss and gathered us together on the couch.

"Today this house is a Boy-Free Zone," she pronounced.

"Right on." Amber likes my mom. No doubt she wishes her mom would declare their house a boy-free zone now and then, instead of dragging home one loser after another.

Mom went on decisively. "For the next twelve hours we'll exercise our right to watch endless chick flicks, eat mounds of popcorn, drink gallons of hot chocolate, apply senseless beauty products, and generally behave like shallow idiots."

She put an arm around me, and I managed a gloomy little smile.

So, that's what we did. I have to admit, Mom's prescription beat the long hours of phone-staring, e-mail-checking, and diary-scribbling I would have indulged in if left to my own devices. Not that I stayed away from those temptations entirely. Ben didn't make any effort to communicate, though, and our Boy-Free Zone remained pure. When we ordered a pizza, Amber asked the guy on the phone to please send a female delivery person if possible. We lived like nuns—well, if nuns wore pajamas all day, snarfed extra-large pepperoni pizzas, and worshiped Adam Brody, that is.

We were popping our fourth bowl of popcorn when Amber showed signs of romantic-comedy-induced delirium. Out of nowhere, she asked Mom, "Are you and Mungo going to get married?"

"It's not in our immediate plans." Mom looked sort of skittish, and snuck a glance at me. "Maybe someday, but not right now."

"That's cool. I don't really believe in marriage anyway," Amber said.

Mom put a bowl of butter into the microwave. "What do you mean?"

"It seems so naive. One person for the rest of your life? I don't think human beings are made for that."

When the microwave beeped, Mom took the butter out and drizzled it over the popcorn, looking thoughtful. "I think it's about finding the right person. With the wrong guy, marriage can be a nightmare. With the right one, though, it could be great."

"Yeah, but that's the thing," I said. "How can you tell the right guy from the wrong guy?"

Amber looked all dreamy, and I could tell she was thinking of Mr. Sands. "You just know."

"Wait, I thought you didn't believe in marriage!" I said.

"Marriage, no. Love, yes."

I couldn't help but think it was ridiculous for Amber to say she's in love with Mr. Sands. I mean, really! The guy couldn't be more wrong for her. Jeremy, on the other hand, is perfect, but she totally overlooks him. Is that just human nature? Do we always gravitate toward the fantasy guy over the flesh-and-blood human being?

"There's a lot that goes into finding the right person," Mom said. "It's not just about attraction. You have to fit, you know? Not just your personalities, but your lifestyles, the things you like to do—everything. Not that you have to be the same person, but it's more complicated than just finding someone you think is sexy."

I didn't want to think about Ben, but I couldn't help it. Did we fit? If we did, how had things gotten so messed up? I remember thinking last night that he and Sophie looked more like a couple than he and I ever had. They were both so gorgeous and elegant. Maybe that was just me being inse-cure, though. Maybe if I believed in myself more, we could fit again. Now I've totally blown it, though, leaving him wide open for Sophie to dig her claws in.

"Mungo, for example. He has to fit with our family—I can't just think about how I feel." Mom's words jolted me out of my morbid shame spiral.

I looked over and her eyes locked on mine. "What do you mean?"

"If you really didn't like him, it wouldn't be a perfect fit. How could I marry someone you despise?"

Amber laughed, but it was a hard, unhappy sound. "Wish *my* mom thought like that. Not that she ever marries the ass-wipes—sorry, Mrs. Sloan, the *jerks*—she hooks up with. I hate every one of them, but she doesn't care."

It hadn't really occurred to me that Mom was worried about me liking Mungo. I mean, yeah, I guess it makes sense when I stop to consider, but I hadn't thought it through.

"Don't worry," I said to Mom. "Mungo's cool. So far. Of course, he's still on probation."

"That's right," Amber said. "Make him work for it."

Monday, February 16
8:20 P.M.

Okay, worst Monday ever? Try this on for size:

1) Wake up with massive zit in third eye position. We're talking deep, painful furuncle (SAT word—useful!).

2) Skate to school, spot BB near front entrance, attempt an ollie in the parking lot, land in scummy puddle and go through entire day with slimy socks.

3) Endure every class with assigned seats watching SDL passing notes to BB.

4) During one class without assigned seats, hold breath

wondering if BB will sit nearby. Feel like heart is being carved out with X-Acto knives as BB chooses seat near SDL instead.

5) Consider faking brain damage to get transferred out of the AP track.

6) After sixth period, run into BB near lockers. Literally. Apologize profusely for damage to his nose.

7) Try not to cry when said collision does nothing to end conversational stalemate.

I realize I'm not the only girl in the history of the world to endure a Monday after a Saturday night breakup. Probably at this very moment there are millions of us sitting in our rooms, crying into our cookie dough ice cream, fighting the urge to text the ex. All the same, it sucks.

So when Amber interrupted my ice cream therapy session with an excited gasp, I was all ears.

"We have to go! We *have* to!" She spun around in the desk chair and looked at me, her eyes bright, her cheeks flushed.

"Go where?"

"Open mike, this Saturday, downtown. *Please?* Please say you'll go?"

"Why? What's the big deal?"

She flung herself onto my bed so she was right beside me. "Rex is reading his poetry! It's a chance to see into his soul!"

Yeah, I thought, *and possibly make out with him in the parking lot afterward.* I didn't want to be snarky, though. She looked so happy and exhilarated. Is it a doomed mission? Sure. But when has that ever stopped us?

"Okay," I sighed. "I'll go."

She broke into a grin so radiant, it lit up her whole face. "G, you know you're the best friend ever?"

"Yeah," I grumbled. "So I hear."

Tuesday, February 17
7:50 P.M.

Peace in Amberland never lasts long. At Triple Shot Betty's this afternoon, she was in full-on viper mode. Beware the caffeinated beast.

I wasn't exactly in a sunny state myself. For starters, Amber is constantly borrowing my clothes, and afterward, instead of hanging them up, she simply surrenders them to the growing miasma of discarded outfits covering every surface of my room. It's getting so I can't even think in there! My *room*, the place that once served as a rare refuge in this godforsaken world, is now a wilderness of dirty laundry.

All the same, I have to admit that having Amber as a live-in best friend has been kind of useful during this post-breakup period. Yes, she's annoying, and sure, she's a horrible roommate, but at least I have someone to talk to when I'm itching to send Ben an e-mail that will surely cement my status as pathetic, groveling dumped-girl extraordinaire.

Amber had just given the hippie chick from the health food store her soy chai latte when she spun around and spat out, apropos of nothing, "Look, just admit it: I'm stupid."

Things were pretty slow, and I was making myself a mocha during the lull. I turned to her, shocked at this non sequitur. "What? Of course you're not stupid."

"You *say* that." She waved a hand dismissively. "But I know I am."

"What brought this on?"

She slumped onto the stool, hiding behind her hair. "I got a D on my expository essay. I'm in bonehead English, and I got a D!"

"Did you put a lot of work into it?"

"No. I did it like ten minutes before class. But if I was smart, I wouldn't have to work at it, right?"

I turned back to my mocha-in-progress. "Amber, you see how much time I put into my homework."

She sighed. "Yeah. And in a couple years, you'll be at Yale or wherever and I'll be . . . I don't know . . . pumping gas."

"You'll be a tattoo artist, right? Isn't that what you want?"

She picked up her sketchbook from its usual place on the counter and started flipping though it listlessly. "I don't know."

"What do you mean, you don't know?"

"This whole thing with Rex . . . it's got me thinking. I mean, I love Floating World and I love tattoos, but maybe I shouldn't limit myself, you know? Maybe I should go to college."

I thought about that for a second. Junior year seemed kind of late in the game to suddenly decide you're college-bound, but then again, people change their plans a lot later than that and sometimes it works. Mom has a friend who managed a hair salon until she was thirty-five, then suddenly decided to be a doctor. Now she's an intern at the local hospital. When you look at it like that, Amber's getting a huge head start.

"If you want to go to college, you'll figure out a way," I said.

She looked at me. "Really?"

"Of course. Even if you don't get in straight out of high school, there's always the JC."

She looked down at her sketchbook, hiding behind her hair again. "You really think that graphic novel I showed you is any good?"

Something clicked in my brain then. Maybe it should have been obvious before, but all at once I realized something: Amber's an artist. I can't really see her as an academic—she's about as analytical as daytime TV—but it was easy to picture her studying art. "Your graphic novel is amazing! You could totally go to art school. That would be perfect. And who says you have to choose between tattoos and college? You could put yourself through school by doing tattoos on the side, right?"

She looked at me, hope lighting up her eyes. "That's true. I could do both, huh?"

For the first time in days, I felt almost happy. Sure, I still have a zit the size of Mt. Fuji and my eyebrows look like a couple of twist-ties glued to my forehead—oh, and I totally blew it with the only guy I've ever really liked—but I'm a good friend. That's something, right?

I heard a car drive up and turned around to see Sophie De Luca in her sparkling Merc with Marcy Adams riding shotgun. Good-bye, tentative sense of well-being. Amber and I exchanged a look. I slid open the window and stared Sophie down.

"Hi there. What can I get you?"

She tossed her hair over her shoulder and glanced down at her cell. "Two double macchiatos, please."

"Coming right up." I punched their order into the register while Amber started brewing their shots. "That will be six fifty, please."

Sophie reached into her Gucci bag, extracted a twenty from her wallet, and handed it to me. Then she held her phone out to Marcy and said in a disgustingly jovial voice, "Benedict is so sweet. Look at this picture he just sent me."

Marcy took the cell from Sophie, studied it a second, and burst out laughing. "Oh my God! That's so adorable!"

I swallowed hard as bile rose in my throat. I could just see myself projectile vomiting right out the window and into Sophie's face; admittedly, her squeals of disgust would be gratifying, but such a stunt would only hasten my descent into Loser Land.

As Amber steamed the milk for their macchiatos, she leaned in and whispered, "Macchiato con loogie for Miss Bitch Face?"

I shook my head. Sure, watching Sophie sip spit might be fun, but I had to hold on to what little dignity I had left. That's how it is when you've been dumped. You have to pick up the jagged shards of your self respect and glue them back together piece by piece.

"Here's your change." I handed the bills and quarters over, trying to keep my expression perfectly neutral. "And here are your drinks."

"Thanks."

No tip. Naturally.

"Hey, what happened to you on Saturday, anyway? You just took off." Sophie handed Marcy her drink and sipped delicately from hers. Even so, I could see her little smirk. "Didn't you have a good time?"

That was it. Good-bye, dignity. "Actually, I got a little tired of watching you throw yourself at my boyfriend."

"Oh, that's too bad," she said, her voice dripping with fake concern. "Except he's *not* your boyfriend anymore, is he?"

I wanted to fire a good comeback—God, I wanted it so badly I could taste it! Instead, I stood there completely paralyzed, as if she'd just punched me in the solar plexus.

Amber nudged me out of the way. "You want a piece of this, you spoiled little Merc-driving bitch? 'Cause if you mess with G, you're going to tangle with me too! You got that?"

"Oooh, very intimidating." You could tell she was trying to sound sarcastic, but the slight wobble in her voice undermined the effect.

Her cell rang, and she looked past Amber to me as she answered it. "Hi, Benedict. Love that picture. . . . Sure. We can be there in five minutes." She waved at us with just the tips of her fingers, shifted gears, and drove away with a devilish little smile.

"I can take her." Amber craned her neck to watch her go.

"No." The adrenaline started to ebb, and in its place I felt a bone-crushing sadness. "Let it go."

9:20 P.M.

> To: Herolovespink@gmail.com
> From: skatergirl@yahoo.com
> Subject: Sophie De Luca is Satan
>
> Hero,
> Grrrr! Sophie De Luca is el Diablo in the flesh! I can't
> believe Ben is even friends with her. Ben and I broke up on
> Saturday and now she's clinging to him like—like a hideous
> clinging thing! Okay, rage is stunting my vocabulary, but
> come on, this is serious. She's driving around in her oh-so-
> pretty Mercedes, flashing me triumphant looks and dropping
> snide little comments. Is he seriously going out with that
> Prada-clad harpy?
>
> Hope you and Claudio are faring better than we are.
> Maybe you're onto something with this long-distance
> relationship thing. No need for birth control, plenty of time
> for homework, and all your beautiful rivals are a continent
> away.
>
> Geena

10:15 P.M.

> To: skatergirl@yahoo.com
> From: Herolovespink@gmail.com
> Subject: RE: Sophie De Luca is Satan

Geebs,
Um, hello?! You and Ben BROKE UP? And I'm just
now hearing about it? You're fixating on Sophie De Luca's
Mercedes while Ben is probably out there somewhere
brokenhearted? I beg of you, for the sake of cousinly love,
forget about your so-called "beautiful rival" and work it out
with Ben directly. Doesn't he deserve that much?

Kisses,
Hero

Wednesday, February 18

3:45 P.M.

So sixth-period English just ended, right? I gathered my
books, minding my own business, trying with monk-like
serenity to elevate my consciousness above Sophie De
Luca's infuriatingly coquettish giggle trailing after Ben, when
suddenly I heard my name.

"Geena?" Mr. Sands's gray eyes were fixed on me. "Can I
speak with you for a moment?"

My heart rumbaed around my ribcage. "Yeah, sure."

I saw Ben glance back at us, and the flicker of jealousy in
his face made me want to run after him, but I didn't.

Mr. Sands waited until the last nosy gawker had left the
room. Then he closed the door, walked over and sat on the
edge of his desk, his hands stuffed in the pockets of his jeans.
Mr. Sands is the only teacher I can think of who wears jeans
on a regular basis. I generally try not to notice how adorable
his butt looks in them when he writes on the board, though

since Ben and I broke up, I let myself indulge more often. It's one of the few real pleasures I have left.

"First, let me just tell you what an excellent job you did on your Camus essay. It had a compelling thesis and very convincing support points."

Compelling, I thought. *He thinks my thesis is compelling!*

"You're very perceptive," he said, scooting back a little, getting more comfortable on the desk. "You know that, right?"

I could feel my cheeks burning, but I tried to keep my voice normal when I said, "I don't know . . . I guess," like an idiot.

He tilted forward slightly and said in a soft, confiding tone, "You're so perceptive that I want to ask your opinion on something."

"Okay." I was hypnotized by his very proximity.

"It's about your coworker, Amber. I'm a little concerned about her right now. She doesn't seem to be herself lately."

"What do you mean?"

"Jeez, this is kind of uncomfortable for me." He let out his breath and ran a hand through his hair. "I've never taught before, you know, so I'm not used to being the 'authority figure.'" The way he said it, I could hear the quotes around it.

"Don't worry," I said. "You can be normal."

I couldn't look directly at his face for too long. I glanced at the posters on the walls, the bookshelves, then at him; out the window, at my shoes, back at him again. I knew I probably looked furtive and childish, but prolonged eye contact was too risky at this range.

"Well, she sent me a message the other day. It just didn't

sound like her at all. She's a lit major at Brown, for God's sake. I mean, this message made her seem . . ." He shifted slightly on the desk. "I don't want to sound like a snob, but frankly, she came off as profoundly uneducated."

My facial muscles tightened. "Really?"

"She even said she's interested in graphic novels. I know they're all the rage right now, but come on, why would a girl like her waste time on comic books?"

"Oh. Yeah." I could feel my mouth drying up. Where was he going with this?

"And then I thought, you know, people make stuff up on the Internet all the time."

My heart went from a rumba to a manic break dance. I felt kind of dizzy, but I forced myself to breathe normally. "True."

"Maybe this Amber isn't the real Amber." He gazed at me with piercing intensity. "Maybe she's an imposter."

"Well . . ." I wiped my sweaty palms on my jeans. "It's possible. I guess."

"Maybe someone hacked into the real Amber's MySpace account and started sending me these silly, poorly spelled messages, trying to convince me it's her. She probably doesn't even know it's happening." He grinned. "I'm sure she'd be mortified to learn that someone is saying she loves graphic novels! You know Amber. She's all about the classics."

I tried to wrap my mind around this madness. He was worried about the real Amber impersonating the fake Amber! Good God . . .

"And then I thought, well, Geena must know Amber pretty well. She works with her. They share so many interests. She

can tell me if the Amber she works with is into Brontë or"—
he snickered—"graphic novels."

I swallowed hard. "Maybe she likes both."

He raised a skeptical eyebrow. "Believe me. This is not the
same person I was communicating with a week ago."

What should I say? How could I possibly get out of this?
The truth just didn't seem like an option. I couldn't do that to
Amber, not like this. And even if she'd forgive me, how could
I look my English teacher in the eye and tell him I'd been
seducing him all along?

"See, the thing is . . ." I looked wildly around the room,
searching for inspiration. There was a flyer for the poetry
reading Saturday, a black-and-white picture of Neal Cassidy
and Jack Kerouac, a bunch of Mrs. Bricker's old posters of
penguins and mountains with stupid slogans like "Believe!"
God, there was nothing. My brain spun like a top. Amber
never even told me she was writing to him on her own. Why
would she do that?

Then I saw it. Over near the door was an old movie poster
for *The Three Faces of Eve*, one of Mom's favorite movies. Bingo!
"Amber wouldn't want me to tell you this, but she suffers from
multiple personality disorder."

I think he was trying to decide if I was joking. "Oh-
kay . . ."

"She's totally embarrassed by it, but she's trying to face
it. That's the real reason she left Brown. It was just getting
worse there."

"I thought her mom was sick." He looked confused.

"Her mom has it too. It's hereditary." I had no idea if
that was true, but he didn't call me on it, so I babbled on.

"She'll be so upset if she finds out I told you. See, one of her personalities is really into graphic novels and another one is into Brontë. It makes perfect sense that both of them would contact you. When she was at Brown her professors freaked whenever she turned in a paper written by the wrong Amber." Okay, that was officially the most ridiculous statement ever to pass through my lips.

"I can see why." I couldn't read his expression.

"Anyway, I've got to go—I'm late for . . . doing homework." I started backing toward the door and tripped over a chair. It clattered to the floor. My hands felt like huge baseball mitts as I tried to set it upright. "Okay. Glad we had this chat. Bye."

I ducked out of his room and darted for my locker. *Glad we had this chat?!* Things were more messed up than ever! I was already dreading the "chat" I'd be forced to have with Amber in a matter of hours.

9:45 P.M.

While Amber was at Floating World, I hacked into her MySpace account and read the messages between her and Mr. Sands. Of course, it felt a little sneaky, but I told myself it was for the greater good. There were only three messages, but I couldn't help cringing at the damage she'd managed to inflict.

> *From: Amber*
> *Date: February 14*
> *Subject: Happy V-Day!*

Hey there, Rex! I'm thinking about u and yr hawt bod today! Have a good one!
(Here she'd pasted a picture of an ornate heart tattooed onto someone's heart-shaped butt.)

From: Rex
Date: February 15
Subject: ???

Umm . . . thanks?

From: Amber
Date: February 16
Subject: Hola Rexito!

Did you not like my V-Day massage? Oh well. No worries. Check out this link to graphic nvls pg: www. grphcnvlsrus.com. It has the most awsome artwork. I no you like books and art so u will love this!!!

God, it was worse than I'd imagined. No wonder Mr. Sands was freaking out. She sounded like one of those creepy viral marketing people who try to friend you all the time on MySpace so they can send you poorly spelled pitches begging you to join their pyramid schemes. I thought of everything we'd done to build up her image as an intellectual: her masterful profile; the subtle, artfully crafted messages; the text-message-prompted date. She'd taken a hatchet to all of that with a handful of ineptly constructed sentences. For a minute I just sat there, staring at my monitor in mute horror.

I actually jumped when Amber walked in.

"What are you doing?" She was immediately suspicious.

I faced her, feeling simultaneously guilty and betrayed. "You've been writing to him."

"Yeah. So?" She marched over to my laptop and closed it. "Why are you even looking at that?"

"How come you didn't . . . ?" I hesitated.

"Didn't what?"

"You know—ask for help."

Her jaw dropped. "Geena! You're the one who's been telling me you want out. What did you say? 'I can't be smart for you all the time'?"

Hearing my words tossed back at me like that prompted a major stab of guilt. I'd used her desperate need to live out my own fantasy. I complained the whole time, but when she cut me loose I resented it. What kind of friend did that?

Amber plopped down onto the bed, looking sad all of a sudden. She smoothed the comforter with her palm. "I'm screwing it up, huh?"

"No!" Yes, but I couldn't tell her that, could I?

"He thinks I'm an ass-face, huh?"

"Amber!" I scooted my desk chair closer. "Don't even say that."

She scowled. "I hate that I'm not as smart as you."

"Listen to me: You're every bit as smart as me—smarter, maybe. It's just that we express ourselves in different ways. You're arty and wild and tough and funny. You've totally got your own style. I'm good at writing; you're good at art. You saw me trying to make that stupid valentine for Ben—I'm hopeless when it comes to drawing."

She laughed a little. "Yeah."

"Yeah! And maybe you're not in AP classes, but who cares? You've got so much going for you. If he can't see that, then he's not right for you."

She looked at me. "So I did screw it up, huh?"

"Um . . . well."

"Just be honest."

I took a deep breath. "Here's the thing: Mr. Sands asked me about you today at school. He thinks there's an Amber-imposter."

Her face scrunched up in confusion.

"His theory is that the Amber we created to make him like you is the real Amber, and the girl sending him messages lately is . . . not really you."

"Wow." She shook her head. "That's so twisted."

"I know, isn't it? But wait, it gets worse. This was probably the wrong thing to do, but I sort of panicked. See, there's this poster in his room for *The Three Faces of Eve*, and it gave me this idea—"

"*The Three Faces of Eve?*"

Obviously I was losing her, so I cut to the chase. "I told him you have multiple personality disorder."

"Like I'm schizophrenic?"

"Technically, I think that's the wrong term—"

"You told him I'm schizo?!" She looked horrified. "And this helps because . . . ?"

"I needed to explain why your new messages are so different. What else could I do, tell him the truth?"

She just sat there, her face going through complex calculations for a long moment. Finally her eyes settled on a look of firm resolve. "You know what? I'm sick of pretending."

"Really?"

"I'm going to tell him the truth."

"The truth?" This was amazing. I couldn't keep the shock out of my voice.

"Yeah."

"Are you serious?"

"Look, I started writing him without you because I realized I was being selfish. I mean, I know you crush on Rex, and that was part of why you helped me—"

I opened my mouth to protest, but she went on.

"Which was okay with me, really! But then it started messing with you and Ben. It was like you were with Ben, but you were also with Rex in this weird way. As much as I needed your help, I finally got that you were right. You couldn't be smart for me all the time; I have to do it on my own. Otherwise I'll screw everything up."

I thought about it. "So, you're going to tell him it was me writing messages for you, and you're not a college student— the whole thing?"

"I can just tell him 'a friend' wrote those messages; I don't have to say it was you. But, yeah, I'll explain that I'm not at Brown and I've never read Brontë and I love tattoos and I'm working on a graphic novel. Come as you are. No disguises."

"What about you being in high school?"

She shrugged. "I guess I'll admit that too. Or maybe not. I don't know. If it comes up. Shit, I might have to."

I thought about it. Whatever shot she had at getting close to him would be obliterated, of course, but was that really a bad thing? They were the most mismatched human beings on the planet. At least this way he could reject her openly and she could move on. Also, I wouldn't have to keep getting tangled in their web of deceit.

"No more wigs, at least," I said.

She picked up the blond Farrah Fawcett one and made a face. "I might have to burn this one."

"Good. I'm scared it might be home to a colony of fleas."

She laughed. Her smile faded almost immediately, though. "You think he'll run screaming from the real me?"

"Well, the real you could get him arrested."

She hugged herself. "This sucks."

"But I think it's the right thing to do." I felt relief flooding through me already.

"I'm going to tell him Saturday. At the poetry reading. You're still coming with me, right?"

I squeezed her arm. "Of course. I've got your back, chica."

"Thanks." She looked like she might cry again, but instead she forced a brave smile. "I'm going to need it."

Friday, February 20
6:45 P.M.

Today in history Ben sat near Sophie again, which made me want to retch, as usual. Several times I caught him sneaking glances at me, though—quick furtive looks that stirred little whirlpools of giddiness inside my stomach. Once, while Ms. Boyle was going on about JFK and the grassy knoll, he looked and I looked at exactly the same moment. I swear to God it was like an invisible force field crackled between us.

When class was over and everyone started the AP march

toward English I stayed at my desk a little longer, taking my time as I put my pen into the front pocket of my bag, then carefully zipped my books and binder into the main compartment. A shadow inched its way onto my desk. When I looked up, there he was, staring down at me with his dark, liquid eyes. It occurred to me then that since we'd broken up he'd become more heartbreakingly familiar and also surprisingly foreign, the way your room does when you've been away from it for a few weeks.

"Hey, Sloane. How's it going?"

He was as gorgeous as usual, except I noticed that there were subtle, bruise-colored half moons under his eyes, like he hadn't been sleeping much.

"I'm good. You?"

"Yeah," he said. "You know. All right." He didn't sound all right, though. It was like all the air had been siphoned from his lungs, leaving him with flat, airless words.

Suddenly I wanted to back up and erase my fake-perky tone, admit to him that since he dumped me every day has been a different shade of gray. I couldn't do that, though. Things were humiliating enough already.

"How's, um . . . ?" Oh God, I couldn't think of what to ask him. I needed my brain to spit out a simple, innocuous, polite sort of question, one that wouldn't make him feel sorry for me or freak him out—just normal small talk. Everyone knows guys hate "talking through feelings" after they've given some girl the boot. I couldn't stand it if he thought I was about to corner him into one of *those* conversations. "How's Mr. Peabody?"

The corners of his mouth twitched as he fought a full-on smile. "He's good. He asked about you the other day."

My heart expanded, in spite of my efforts to stay calm. "Really?"

"Yeah, he was all, 'Ruff-ruff, arr-ruff ruff!'"

"Wow! He's so expressive."

"Not really." He looked at his shoes, then back up at me. "Actually, he's pretty bad at saying what he needs to say."

"You coming, or what?"

I turned to see Sophie in the doorway. She had on red patent-leather boots and a saucy black dress with trim that matched her shoes perfectly. Her dark hair was pulled into a messy French twist, just the right amount of fringe left dangling about her face for a vaguely tousled effect. She looked disgustingly perfect. I wanted to throw something at her.

Ben opened his mouth to speak, but the late bell rang, cutting him off. I felt like grabbing his hand and running out the door, down the hall, and out to the parking lot so we could drive off in his Volvo, go find a quiet place to park like we did that day in the rain, just talk and kiss and never hurt each other again.

Instead, I said, "We'll get a tardy in English."

"Yeah." He shot me one last burning look. "We'd better go."

Saturday, February 21
4:20 P.M.

Amber and I had just downed three shots of espresso each to wake ourselves up this morning when suddenly there was an onslaught of customers—way more than usual. We churned out lattes, cappies, chais, and mochas like a human vending machine. When it finally slowed down around nine we were exhausted and jacked at the same time, running on a potent mix of adrenaline, caffeine, and sleep deprivation. We cranked up the James Brown and danced like fiends, cracking each other up with our increasingly bizarre renditions of the funky chicken.

After we'd laughed so hard we couldn't possibly laugh any more, Amber sat on the stool and her face got unexpectedly serious. "I talked to my mom yesterday. She kicked Danny out. I guess I'm moving back home."

For a giddy moment, all I could see was me in my room all alone with everything just the way I liked it: my books lined up neatly on their shelves, my clothes and shoes all returned to their rightful places in the closet. But then I thought of Amber back in her house, and I felt a little less thrilled.

"Are you sure? Is he definitely out of the picture?"

"Yeah. He got a job in Miami. There'll be an entire country between us, thank God."

"How's your mom doing?" Translation: *Are you sure you want to go back to that boozy bag?* Not to be mean, but Amber's mom isn't winning any prizes in the parental category this month.

She considered. "Pretty good, actually. I don't know what your mother told her that night when she came over, but whatever it was, seems like it sank in. She's all into being a better mom now." Her smile was cynical, but I could see little glimmers of hope in there too. "We'll see how long that lasts."

"Good. I'm glad she's making an effort."

Amber turned around and started making herself a latte. I couldn't imagine ingesting another drop of caffeine—I felt like the Energizer bunny already. "Are you seriously having more?"

She looked at the cup in her hand, which trembled slightly. "Maybe I should make it decaf."

I heard a car behind me and turned to see Jeremy Riggs cruising up to the window. His rusty old Mercury idled there, wheezing translucent blue clouds of exhaust. A shy, mischievous smile bloomed on his lips as I leaned out the window toward him.

"Jeremy! Whattup?" I was happy to see him.

"Hey, Geena. How's it going?" He dropped his voice to a near-whisper and tried to see around me. "Is Amber back there?"

"Sure. Why?"

"You ever seen the movie *Say Anything?*"

"Yeah! Cameron Crowe, right? I love that cheeseball eighties stuff."

"Well, I'm about to put its cheeseball powers to the test."

I had no idea what he meant, but I didn't have time to ask. Amber came over to say hello then. She'd just barely opened her mouth when Jeremy flew into action. He hoisted an old paint-splattered boom box out the window and pushed PLAY. Peter Gabriel's "In Your Eyes" blared from the speakers so loudly, we both took half a step back, startled. He sat there, wordlessly gazing at Amber, his pale, skinny arms straining under the weight of the CD player.

Before the song was over, another car drove up behind him. I tore my eyes away from Jeremy long enough to check out who it was. Oh, *sacrebleu*, it was Lane, our boss! He sat in his green MINI Cooper with his arms folded, a distinctly unhappy expression brewing behind his enormous Wayfarers.

"What is this?" he shouted. "Serenade Saturday?! Give him his coffee and say buh-bye, girls!"

Jeremy hastily stashed his boom box on the seat beside him and tore out of the parking lot. Amber and I just stood there, our mouths hanging open. When Lane pulled up and saw us like that he just about blew a fuse.

"Do I pay you girls to *flirt*? Do I? Can we run a business on romance?"

"No, Lane." I shook off my surprise and focused on his disgruntled face. "Sorry. What can I get you?"

"You know perfectly well what you can get me! A double cappuccino, wet." Lane's bark is worse than his bite. He knows I'm the only Triple Shot Betty who can make his cappies just the way he likes them. As long as that's true, I've got long-term job security.

While I made his drink, he calmed down enough to ask, "Which one of you girls was that little twerp serenading, anyway?"

"Her," I said, pointing at Amber.

"Well, don't let that one go," he advised her. "He may not look like much now, but it's always the nerdy ones who end up making bank after high school. The quarterback will be bald, paunchy, and working for his dad's construction companies in ten years—trust me."

"He's great, isn't he?" I enthused.

"Seems very romantic. What more could you want?"

I elbowed Amber. "Thank you! That's what I keep telling her."

"Yeah, yeah, yeah," Amber grumbled. "If you both love him so much, why don't *you* go out with him?"

Lane smirked. "I'd be arrested, honey."

"Besides," I said, leaning out to hand Lane his drink. "He doesn't want us. He wants you."

Sunday, February 22
12:30 A.M.

At what point did I realize with absolute certainty that God hates me? Oh, gee, let me think about that . . . I'd say the moment I walked into La Plaza Cafe and saw Ben Bettaglia sharing a table with Sophie De Luca.

Yep, that'd be the moment.

Who knew an open mike would draw such a crowd? Everyone was there: the stofers, PJ, Marcy Adams, Jeremy and all of his band mates, plus scores of terminally hip twentysomethings, some of whom I recognized from Floating World. Ben and Sophie were sitting at a table with PJ and Marcy, so they *might* not be on what could be called an actual *date*, but the second Sophie saw me she tossed her hair in a *très* annoying fashion and leaned over to whisper something into *Benedict's* ear.

I had to hold myself back, I'm telling you.

"Okay," Amber coached me, leading me by the elbow to a table on the opposite side of the room. "This looks bad, I see that, but stay cool. If Ben's doing her, he's not half as perfect for you as I thought."

I kept my expression as blank as possible, in spite of the overwhelming urge to retch.

"Are you all right?" Amber handed me a napkin. "Looks like you're sweating a little."

"I'm fine," I lied, dabbing at my forehead. It was bad enough seeing Sophie trying to steal Ben back when we were together. Now, though, knowing I had no claim on him and she had every right to move in for the kill, I found the sight almost unbearable.

Amber scanned the room. "Rex isn't here yet."

"Maybe we should just go," I croaked.

"Let's give him ten minutes." Her tone was imploring and uncharacteristically sympathetic. "I know it's hard. Do you mind? I won't make you if you can't handle it."

I willed myself not to look at their table, but found myself sneaking a quick peek anyway. They weren't touching; that was promising, right? Just then, as if reading my thoughts, Sophie cupped a hand around Ben's ear and whispered something. I wanted to strangle her. Never in my life had violence seemed like such a logical solution.

"I can handle it," I said, barely getting the syllables out.

"You sure?"

I nodded. "If I suddenly leap across the room and try to claw her eyes out, promise you'll restrain me."

"Yeah, okay. She's got it coming, though. Look at how smug she is."

"Amber? You're not helping."

"You're right," she said. "Give peace a chance."

Right then Mr. Sands walked in. He had on faded jeans and a camel-colored suede shirt open at the collar. His hair was slicked back—a look I'd never seen on him. He walked with a beat poet cool, assessing the room with a sly, knowing squint.

I thought I heard Amber suck in her breath. Then again, it could have been a collective gasp coming from every female in that room, and probably a few of the guys too. He sure knew how to make an entrance.

A little woman in a knit poncho and leopard print glasses stepped up to the mike, holding a coffee mug. I thought I recognized her as a cashier from Body and Soul Natural Foods. She wore her long gray hair coiled into Princess Lea buns. To be honest, though, her face looked a lot more like Yoda, all squat and jowly and slightly yellow, with grooves in her forehead so deep, they reminded me of an accordion.

"Hellooooo everyone," she purred into the mike. "Glad to see such a fabulous turnout. This is our first monthly Saturday Night Sonoman Poetry Series. It's open mike, anyone can sign up, and the list is over there with my son Ronnie."

She nodded at a tall, skinny guy by the door. He sported bleached, randomly hacked hair, as if he'd done it himself with a bottle of Clorox and a pair of child's scissors.

"We ask that all poets keep their readings to five minutes or less," Ms. Yoda went on. "Other than that, it's up to you. Just try to speak into the mike and enunciate. Ronnie, who do we have up first?"

Ronnie consulted his list. "DJ-PJ?"

Ms. Yoda scanned the room, with her mouth puckered slightly as if she'd discovered a fly in her coffee. "Is *DJ-PJ* here?"

PJ swaggered up to the mike and cradled it like a pro. "I'm requesting a little backup on this number. Dog? You guys down?"

All three stofers popped up from their table and sauntered over to PJ in a pack, looking stoned as usual. They arranged themselves behind him like a trio of backup singers for some Motown headliner. Responding to a wordless cue from PJ, they simultaneously cupped their hands around their mouths and started in on a steady beat, bobbing their scruffy heads in unison. PJ leaned into the mike, his body moving instinctively to the rhythm.

"I ain't no Shakespeare
I know the stakes here
I gotta rhyme if I want a place here,
I'm not your Kipling,
That's not a bad thing,
I got the grooves of a mother-f-ing rap king."

The crowd cheered wildly at that. I glanced over at Ms. Yoda in time to see the wrinkles between her brows furrow even deeper. PJ had tactfully implied the curse without actually saying it, but apparently she didn't know how lucky she was.

"I know the score,
I see the door,
But I won't go there if you want more."

Again, the audience burst into an explosion of rowdy cheers. Unable to stop myself, I glanced over at Ben; his dark eyes met mine, and for a second I felt light-headed.

"We're through with V-Day,
But you'll hear me say,
Will you be mine? 'Cause I'm DJ-PJ!"

That was it—everyone went nuts. Of course, Ms. Yoda gave the whole room a sour, disapproving look, but nobody paid her any attention.

After that there was a long string of considerably less interesting poets. A girl with hair the color and texture of a skunk read a rambling free verse thing she called "Ode to Razor Blades." A middle-aged paunchy guy in army fatigues shouted seven anti-war haikus that hurt to listen to. A shy sophomore in a Jim Morrison T-shirt mumbled his way through an unintelligible abstract poem about—as far as I could tell—Final Fantasy XII.

Amber and I were rolling our eyes so often we saw more of the ceiling than anything else. I'm not trying to be mean, but these people were creating a truly persuasive argument for censorship. People should stop worrying so much about their kids being exposed to sex and violence—exposure to bad art is way more traumatic.

At last Ronnie called out "Mr. Rex Sands" and the whole room went dead silent. He strode up to the mike with the same cocksure cool he displayed in the classroom. Why shouldn't he be confident? He's got Brad Pitt good looks and the easy charisma of a man who's treated like a god wherever he goes. Even though the cafe was sauna-like with all those bodies, he showed no signs of breaking a sweat.

Licking his lips a couple of times, smoothing his hair once, he began to read:

"Oh you generations of wine-swilling Sonomans
In a sea of discontent, I can feel you churning
You, the offspring of SUV-driving soccer moms
Your chubby yabie bodies crammed into low-rider jeans
Your stabbing eyes accusing me of what I don't know
But I can tell you for certain, this is not My Space
This is not my Best Small Town in America
no matter what *Time* magazine tells me."

Okay, so it went on like that—I can't remember every word. Basically, he ranted about Sonoma and everyone in it, employing a very *Howl*-like, free-verse style. His tone was snide and condescending. Not a super flattering portrait. Even if you factored out the sting of his elitist sentiments, though, the poem wasn't very good.

Sitting there listening to him, I started to get sort of irritated. Here's this guy Amber and I have been freaking out over for weeks. We've spent hours and hours trying to mold ourselves into his perfect dream girl. Why? What's he got that's so obsession-worthy? He's been sneering at us the whole time, at our "chubby yabie bodies crammed into low-rider jeans." What gives him the right to pass judgment? Why had we given him that power?

"I see you in your coffee shack,
Hot chicks-in-a-box, fast and easy,
Freckled cleavage spilling out the window
Red hair perfumed with cheap shampoo

Eager to fill my cup with rich black drugs
Worshipping me with your kohl-smeared green eyes
Speedy, affordable love, always to go."

I snuck a peak at Amber. She was gnawing on her lower lip, her eyebrows pushed together in a look of pained confusion. I may not have a PhD in literature, but I can tell you what that stanza sounded like to me: He was calling my best friend a coffee-slinging slut. I could see she was headed for the same conclusion.

When he'd finished, there was a smattering of bewildered applause. Ms. Yoda thanked us all for coming. People headed toward the counter for coffee refills. Conversation, at first a low hum, cranked up a few notches in volume. I heard Sophie's annoying, flirty laughter from across the room, but resisted the urge to turn in her direction.

Amber stood up, her jaw set in a hard, determined look I hadn't seen on her in a long time. I've missed that Amber— the in-your-face, uninhibited, who-gives-a-shit girl I'd known and loved before she started trying so hard to be someone else.

"What are you going to do?"

Her eyes had turned a luminous emerald hue that scared me a little. "Set things straight."

"Okay. I'm here if you need back—"

But she was already marching over to Mr. Sands, her bag slung across her chest bandolier style. I stood up and took a few steps in their direction, my curiosity winning out over etiquette. The second she opened her mouth, though, I knew I'd be able to hear their conversation just fine from where I stood.

"Who do you think you are?" Amber's voice cut through the din, and everyone quieted down, smelling blood in the water.

"I'm sorry?" Mr. Sands looked taken aback.

"Just because you have an education, you think that gives you the right to laugh in our faces?"

"Well, I certainly had no intention—"

"You don't even think we get it, do you?" she scoffed. "You figured someone like me would be so ignorant, I'd never even know you were dissing me! What am I good for, anyway? I'm barely even smart enough to pour your coffee."

He glanced around nervously. "Amber, you're not well. I think you're having an episode."

"An episode!"

"Let me guess." He had the audacity to smirk. "Right now, I bet you really like graphic novels."

"Yes! I love graphic novels and tattoos and loud music and I've never read Brontë or Kerouac in my life! Also, I think you're full of shit. I'm embarrassed that I tried so hard to be the kind of girl you'd like." Tears glistened in her eyes; she stared at him like she was seeing him for the first time. "I thought you inspired me to be better—more intellectual—than I was. You didn't. All you did was make me feel stupid." She pivoted away from him and ran out the front door, leaving a trail of scandalized murmurs in her wake.

I started after her, but by the time I got to the sidewalk, she'd already slammed the door of her El Dorado. Her wheels emitted a high-pitched squeal as she tore away from the curb.

"Amber!" I called after her taillights. It was no use, though. Even if she could hear me, she showed no signs of stopping.

I turned back around and pushed open the door of the cafe, only to find everyone staring at me. Somehow, in that moment, everything became clear. I thought of what my dad said, about him and Mom making each other feel small. I saw how Mr. Sands does that to Amber—how everything about him made her want to be somebody she's not. It was never like that with Ben and me. Sophie made me feel small, but Ben got me, he really did, and if I could just get past my insecurities I could start to savor that.

In that moment I was seized by some force I didn't even know was in me. Maybe Amber's dramatic exit made me bold. Maybe all those eyes on me went to my head. Maybe I was drunk with relief knowing our god Mr. Sands had finally plummeted to earth where he belonged. Whatever the reason, I crossed the room as everyone watched and headed straight for Ben. He was still sitting with Sophie, who had scooted her chair so close to his she was practically in his lap.

"Are you going out with her?" I demanded, thrusting a chin at Sophie.

Ben's eyes went wide. "You mean like—"

"Going out—is she your girlfriend?"

"No," he said quietly but firmly.

Sophie made an indignant, strangled sound in her throat.

"Do you miss me?" I asked.

"Uh." He hesitated half a second, and I thought I'd die, but then he smiled. "Yeah, actually."

I put one hand on my hip. "Really? You're not just saying that because everyone's staring at us and you don't want to humiliate me even more than I'm humiliating myself?"

His smile spread. "No, I'm not just saying it."

"Good, because I miss you too." I took a deep breath. "And I'm sorry I let all my stupid insecurities get in the way. I'm not a good girlfriend yet. But maybe I can learn."

He nodded, his face solemn. "I think you're trainable."

That made me laugh. "Will you help me find Amber now?"

Sophie stood up, her blue eyes fixed on me like lasers. "This is so childish!"

"Yeah, I guess I'm childish, but you know what? He likes me better. So sit down, fashion plate."

Astoundingly, she sat. Ben stood. And together, we walked out of that place holding hands.

○ ● ● ○ ● ○

Just as we were climbing into Ben's car, I heard a voice calling my name. I was half afraid it would be Sophie, challenging me to a parking lot brawl, but when I turned around I saw Jeremy, his blue-streaked bangs flopping over his eyes, his skinny legs running after us.

"Can I go with you guys?" He jogged up to us, a little out of breath.

"You sure?" I asked. "She can be a handful when she's in a mood."

"Are you kidding? I live for her moods!"

"Come on," Ben said, "hop in."

It took us a while to find her. She wasn't at her house or mine, she wasn't at Triple Shot Betty's or Baskin-Robbins or any of the other places we could think of. Then Jeremy suggested Floating World, saying he was pretty sure she had her own key. He was right. The El Dorado was in the parking lot, and the back door was unlocked. We found her sitting in the shadowy corner of the closed tattoo parlor, hunched over a lime green coffee table, flipping though the pages of her sketchbook, her face wet with tears.

"Hey." I sat down beside her on the floor. The guys hovered a second, then took a seat on the suede couch nearby.

She looked at me, glanced over at Ben and Jeremy, then back down at her sketchbook. "I guess I'm ass clown of the day, huh?"

I touched her arm. "He doesn't deserve you—he really doesn't. You did the right thing."

She let out a small, humorless laugh. "Yeah. I guess."

"I'm serious." I leaned forward to get a better look at her. "You should be with someone who understands how smart and funny and creative you really are."

"Oh come on, Geena. You're the smart one. I'm just the slut in bonehead classes who's never going to do anything. Everyone knows that."

"You're not a slut. And you can do anything!"

"No!" She turned on me, her expression fierce. "*You* can do anything. Not me."

"How can you say that?"

Fresh tears started streaming down her cheeks, and she smeared them roughly with the heel of her hand. "I'm not going to college. You know that."

"I don't know that, and neither do you."

She breathed out in frustration. "People with education are the haves, Geena—my mom and her boyfriends, they're the have-nots. That's just how it is. They start separating us now. That's why you and I don't have any classes together. The system decided I was stupid."

"Then you have to prove the system wrong."

"It's not that easy. In my house, the Domino's Pizza menu is the closest we come to literature."

"Don't want to interrupt," Jeremy said, and we both turned to him, a little startled. "But I have to. Amber, if you think you're stupid, well, that's just . . . stupid!"

Ben, Amber, and I all laughed, but Jeremy pressed on with earnest determination.

"I mean it. I've been watching you for months and you're fascinating. I never know what you're going to do next. Seriously. So if you think you're stupid, I must be sick." His cheeks burned, but he kept talking. "Which I'm not. So you're not. If that makes any sense. And in my opinion, Mr. Sands is a pretentious dick-wad."

Amber let out a throaty laugh. "I'm starting to figure that out."

"Come on." I tucked a strand of hair behind her ear. "Let's go somewhere and celebrate."

She raised an eyebrow. "What's the occasion?"

"You put Mr. Sands in his place." I glanced at Ben. "And I completely humiliated myself in the name of love."

Her eyes lit up. "Really? How?"

"I'll tell you everything over a sundae." I stood and held out my hand. "Come on. My treat."

She let me pull her to her feet. "I bet I still win the prize for most embarrassing public display of emotion, though."

Ben's eyes sparkled as we all headed for the exit. "I don't know. Sloane here sure gave you a run for your money."

I shoved him out the door. "Thanks a lot! You're the one who drove me to it!"

Amber and Jeremy walked toward the parked cars. I started to follow, but Ben grabbed my hand and pulled me back. All at once I could smell him—that delicious, sweet mixture of boy sweat and his mother's laundry detergent. He kissed me on the lips, gently at first, then more deeply, with an urgency that matched my own. My brain, my lips, every hair follicle exploded with electricity. When the kiss ended, he whispered into my ear, "I missed you so much."

"I missed you too."

"Come on, you guys!" Amber called. "Stop groping! I want my sundae."

We joined them, but not before sneaking in one more quick, spine-tingling kiss.

4:10 P.M.

Amber and I worked our usual shift this morning at TSB. Around nine I heard the familiar harrumph of Ben's ancient Volvo and turned to see his smiling face at the window. Without even thinking I rushed over, leaned way out, and kissed him in greeting.

"Mmmm," he said. "Who needs caffeine when that's on the menu?"

Suddenly I noticed Jeremy riding shotgun. "Oh, hi."

"Hey," he said. "What's up, Geena?"

"What time do you guys get off?" Ben asked. "I just ran into Jeremy downtown and we decided we're taking you Bettys out to dinner."

"Really?" I looked over my shoulder to gauge Amber's reaction. She was making herself another latte, though, and barely looked up.

"We want—well, *I* want—to make up for the disaster of

Valentine's. What do you say?" Ben's face positively glowed. I wanted to kiss him again, but I figured I should show some restraint, seeing as I was officially on the clock.

"I think that sounds great. Amber? You free?"

She looked past Ben and me to Jeremy, who sat there in the passenger seat, his face one big nervous question mark. "Who's asking, exactly?"

"What do you mean?" Jeremy countered, suspicious.

"I mean, Ben's obviously asked Geena out to dinner. Are you asking me?"

He shook his head at her in disbelief. "The first time I asked you out, I sang it in front of the whole school. Last time I was here, I made a total ass of myself with a boom box. I think *you* should ask *me* out for once."

She raised an eyebrow. Then a slow smile spread across her face. "Fair enough. Want to go to dinner?"

He smirked. "Don't mind if I do."

After we'd decided on a time and they'd driven off, I couldn't help myself—I was so excited I started bouncing around Triple Shot Betty like a tweaker on a pogo stick. "Come on, admit it! You totally like him!"

Amber shook her head. "Relax already. It's no big deal. We're just having dinner."

"Okay, okay, but promise me this: If he wants to kiss you tonight, let him."

She rolled her eyes. "I'm not going to kiss Jeremy just because you want me to!"

"All I'm saying is keep an open mind."

She laughed. "My mind is perfectly open. And okay, I admit, he's a tiny bit cute."

I punched the air. "Yes!"

"Maybe even the slightest bit sexy."

I made another fist and punched the doorjamb. "Double yes! Ouch."

"But I'm not jumping into anything this time."

I nodded, suddenly sober. "I totally understand."

"Tonight, possible kiss," she said, her tone measured. "Tomorrow, unreasonable infatuation, total meltdown, major drama. You see? I'm learning to take it slowly."

I put an arm around her. "You're right. You should probably take your time and get to know him."

"Listen to you. Little Miss *Looove* Expert."

"Not an expert, exactly." I smiled. "But I'm learning."

11:55 P.M.

Ben, Amber, Jeremy, and I had a super fun dinner at the Red Grape Pizzeria tonight. Afterward, Jeremy and Amber went to hear some graphic novelist give a talk at Readers Books. Ben and I were overdue for a little tête-à-tête, so we went off on our own after dropping them at the bookstore.

We drove around aimlessly for a little while before I made a split-second decision to take him where no boy has gone before.

"Turn left here," I told him.

He shot me a sideways glance, but followed directions. "Where are we going?"

"Someplace secret." I gave him what I hoped was a Woman of Mystery look. It only got a laugh, though, which wasn't exactly my intention. "Just shut up and drive!"

I showed him where to park, and then I led him down the trail in the moonlight. It was unseasonably warm, and the breeze felt incredibly gentle on my bare arms and face, like silk scarves.

"You're making me nervous, Sloane. Is this where you lure unsuspecting victims and hack them into tiny pieces?"

"Yeah," I laughed. "Just let me grab my chain saw."

When we got to Geevana, we stood together inside the semicircle of oak trees and looked out at the valley below. Everything was silvery-green. Sonoma seemed like one of those toy villages people set up at Christmas—totally peaceful and miniature and sweet, like nothing bad could ever happen there.

"This is my favorite place," I told Ben. "I call it Geevana. I've been coming here since I was eleven. I used to talk to these trees." I patted Albert's low, mossy trunk. "And that rock. In the spring an iris will bloom right here where we're standing."

"It's beautiful." He stood very still, taking it all in.

I felt so relieved, somehow. As absurd as it sounds, I was afraid he wouldn't get it. He did though, I could tell. The way he stood there, scanning the landscape with his eyes, it was obvious he understood this wasn't just someplace to make out; it was my own little sanctuary, and I was sharing it with him.

"I'm sorry I was such an idiot that night at the dance." I didn't dare look at him. "I always act stupid with Sophie. She seems so mature and glamorous, I feel like a troll by comparison."

With one finger, he tilted my face toward his. "You're not a troll."

"You know what I mean. I couldn't help thinking that secretly you wanted to be with her, but you were too nice to tell me."

He tipped his head back and let out a quick, incredulous laugh. "You've got to be kidding! I've told you a million times, I'm not into her like that. I thought you felt that way about Mr. Sands."

I bit my lip. "I did have a tiny crush on him for a while. Things got really messed up. See, Amber wanted him to think she was this über-intellectual college girl. I was sending him messages that were supposed to be from her. The whole thing was ridiculous. He turned out to be a pretentious snob anyway."

"So you did like him . . ." He sounded hurt.

"That whole thing was just a childish fantasy. I was afraid of everything happening between you and me. It was getting so intense. Mr. Sands was just a silly distraction." I slipped my fingers in his and tugged him toward me. "You're the real thing, Ben. I was stupid to let you dump me."

He grinned. Our lips were centimeters apart. "I didn't dump you."

"You did too!"

"I offered you an out and you jumped at the chance."

I let my lips graze his, ever so lightly. "Is that the way you're going to spin it?"

"Uh-huh." He reached into his pocket then, and pulled something out. "Although, I do have some evidence that you liked me that night. I was just a little slow in piecing it together."

I looked down and saw he was holding out a sheet of

folded paper. It was hard to see exactly what it was in the moonlight. I took it from him and examined it more closely. It was the valentine I'd intended to give him, the one I'd torn up and thrown at him! I couldn't believe it. He'd taped it back together, piece by piece, meticulously reconstructing it until it was whole again.

"It was a really great valentine," he said. "Next time, though, you might want to rethink the method of delivery."

I laughed. I was thankful for the darkness, though, since I was also crying.

"Here. I'll trade you." He took the card back from me and handed me a small book.

"What's this?" I stealthily wiped away a tear.

"I, uh, got you this for Valentine's Day. It just never seemed like the right moment to give it to you that night." His voice broke. Was he crying too? "Better late than never though, right?"

I held it close to my face so I could see better. It was a journal—no lines inside, my favorite kind. It was covered in a collage of photos taken over the six months we were together: us at the beach, us at my house, us in front of Triple Shot Betty's. A surge of happiness welled up inside my throat; it was so concentrated I thought I might choke on it.

"Thank you," I told him when I could speak.

"You're welcome. Sorry it took me so long."

I wrapped my arms around his neck and we kissed, the warm breeze whipping through our hair like a mischievous spirit. I could smell dew in the grass and the perfume of singed garlic and grilled meats floating up from the restaurants in the valley below. I wanted to stop time then, so we could stay there on that ridge forever.

When at last we pulled away, he looked down at me with an impish grin. "So you're not going to leave me for Dr. Hipster?"

"Believe me, you've got nothing to worry about."

"That's good." His face went suddenly serious. "You do realize I'm getting an A-plus in his class, and you're just getting a regular A, right?"

"Oh my God!" I pushed him away. "You're such a liar!"

"I hope you're not thinking about extra credit. I'd hate to see you stoop that low."

I started chasing him around the meadow. "That's it! You're dead!"

"After that stunt with Amber, he might even knock you down to a B."

I grabbed hold of his shirt and wrestled him to the ground. When he was pinned beneath me, gasping and panting, he breathed, "Just kidding! I'm sure you'll get a B-plus, at least."

"You laugh now," I warned him, "but when I'm giving the valedictorian speech at graduation, you'll be weeping. You're going to be so sorry when—"

I was going to issue more threats, but he leaned up and stopped my mouth with a kiss.

For once, I didn't complain.

♥